Off Off Broadw[...]
Festival Plays
Thirty-Fourth Series

DROP
by J. Michael DeAngelis & Pete Barry

THE EDUCATION OF MACOLOCO
by Jen Silverman

REALER THAN THAT
by Kitt Lavoie

THE STUDENT
by Matt Hoverman

THUCYDIDES
Scott Elmegreen & Drew Fornarola

JUST KNOTS
by Christina Gorman

A SAMUEL FRENCH ACTING EDITION

SAMUEL FRENCH
FOUNDED 1830

NEW YORK HOLLYWOOD LONDON TORONTO

SAMUELFRENCH.COM

MUSIC USE NOTE

Licensees are solely responsible for obtaining formal written permission from copyright owners to use copyrighted music in the performance of this play and are strongly cautioned to do so. If no such permission is obtained by the licensee, then the licensee must use only original music that the licensee owns and controls. Licensees are solely responsible and liable for all music clearances and shall indemnify the copyright owners of the play and their licensing agent, Samuel French, Inc., against any costs, expenses, losses and liabilities arising from the use of music by licensees.

**IMPORTANT BILLING AND CREDIT
REQUIREMENTS**

All producers of *DROP, THE EDUCATION OF MACOLOCO, REALER THAN THAT, THE STUDENT, THUCYDIDES,* and *JUST KNOTS* must give credit to the Author of the Play in all programs distributed in connection with performances of the Play, and in all instances in which the title of the Play appears for the purposes of advertising, publicizing or otherwise exploiting the Play and/or a production. The name of the Author *must* appear on a separate line on which no other name appears, immediately following the title and *must* appear in size of type not less than fifty percent of the size of the title type.

Dear Friend,

I am pleased to introduce you to the winners of the 34th Annual Samuel French Off Off Broadway Short Play Festival. We are very happy to share these exciting and inventive new plays with you.

For this, our 34th year, the Final Forty Playwrights were chosen from an initial submission pool of 718—more than double the number of applicants for last year's Festival. A diverse group of playwrights hailing from across the US, the UK, and Singapore collaborated with over 30 different production companies and educational institutions to bring their work to the stage. We are grateful to all who gave their time, effort, dedication, and passion to bring their work to the Festival. Each and every playwright and presenting organization should be very proud of their accomplishment, and I would personally like to congratulate and thank them for their participation.

Through this festival we hope to give emerging playwrights something very valuable in addition to their developmental process – exposure. True to this goal, we were happy to bring in a new element to our nightly judging panel. Both local NYC and regional Artistic Directors joined our group of esteemed playwrights and agents as judges. We were extremely grateful for the time and expertise they brought to our adjudication process.

We at Samuel French see our role as a conduit through which playwrights may gain greater exposure to a broader market; enabling those playwrights to connect with theatre students, professionals and audience members all over the world. In the last five years alone, we have licensed over 50 productions of winning Festival plays. In this way, essential building blocks are provided with which each playwright can build a stronger career of greater scope.

The six winning plays of the 2009 Festival presented in this collection represent a wide variety of styles and voices. We feel that the excitement we experienced bringing these works to the stage is infectious, and that you will discover a connection to these energetic and provocative works, bringing them to life on your local stage.

Please enjoy the 34th Off Off Broadway Festival winners!

Sincerely,

Leon Embry
President and C.E.O.
Samuel French, Inc.

34th Annual
SAMUEL FRENCH

Off Off Broadway
Short Play Festival

SAMUEL FRENCH
OOB
FESTIVAL

JULY 14TH-19TH
The Mainstage Theater
NYC

The Samuel French Off Off Broadway Short Play Festival started in 1975 and is one of the nation's most established and highly regarded short play festivals. During the course of the Festival's first 34 years, over 500 theatre companies and schools participated in the Festival, including companies from coast to coast as well as abroad from Canada, Singapore, and the United Kingdom. Over the years, 194 submitted plays have been published, with many of the participants becoming established, award-winning playwrights.

Festival Coordinator: Ken Dingledine
Production Coordinator: Billie Davis
Literary Coordinator: Roxane Heinze-Bradshaw
Assoc. Literary Coordinator/Web Content Editor: Amy Rose Marsh
Press/Public Relations: Cromarty & Company
Visuals/Design: Gene Sweeney
Judge Liaison: Jason Blitman
Webmaster: Phillip DeVita
Lighting Design: Miriam Crowe
Board Operator: Syche Hamilton
Photography: Charley Parden
Festival Crew: Kathryn Appleton, Jordan Barsky, Jenny Bartolf, Amy Cruz, Gavin Davis, Katherine DiSavino, Melody Fernandez, Joe Ferreira, Laura Lindson, Casey McLain, Josephine Messina, Sara Mirowski, Dora Naughton

SAMUEL FRENCH STAFF

Samuel French President & C.E.O.: Leon Embry
Samuel French Vice-President: Abbie Van Nostrand
Rita Maté, **Director of Finance**
Ken Dingledine, **Publications Manager**
Roxane Heinze-Bradshaw, **Managing Editor**
Billie Davis, **Office Manager**
Brad Lohrenz, **Director of Licensing**
Melody Fernandez, **Head of Amateur Licensing**
Lysna Marzani, **Contracts Manager**
Amy Rose Marsh, **Editorial Associate**
Gene Sweeney, **Graphic Designer**

GUEST JUDGES

Charles Busch	Julia Hansen	Jeffrey Rosenstock
Jan Buttram	Jordan Harrison	Jessica Sarbo
Elaine Devlin	William Hayes	Jim Simpson
Seth Glewen	Arthur Kopit	Olivier Sultan
Ron Gwiazda	Leslie Lee	Billy Van Zandt
Evans Haile	Deb Margolin	Derek Zasky

CONTENTS

DROP

by Pete Barry & J. Michael DeAngelis

DROP was originally workshopped at the BRUNCH one act festival at the Actor's Playground Theater in New York City, December 28th & 29th, 2002. It was directed by JoEllen Notte. The cast was as follows:

MIKE. . . . . Justin Schaefers
RIC . . . . Nicholas Carriere
JACKSON. . . . . Morgan Lamarre

DROP premiered at Circle Players Theater in Piscataway, New Jersey as part of an evening titled *An Evening on the Porch,* July 13-27, 2007. It was directed by Pete Barry & J. Michael DeAngelis.

That cast and creative team of that production repeated their roles for the 34th Annual Samuel French Off Off Broadway Short Play Festival production, on July 19th, 2009 at the Mainstage Theatre in New York City:

MIKE. . . . . J. Michael DeAngelis
RIC . . . . Pete Barry
JACKSON. . . . . John P. Dowgin

CHARACTERS

MIKE – Afraid of heights. 20s or early 30s
RICK – Mike's friend. 20s or early 30s
JACKSON – A repair man. Any age.

SET

The front car of a roller coaster, at the top of the largest hill.

The roller coaster can be as realistic or minimalist as desired by the production designer. It can be successfully represented by nothing more than two chairs or in a fuller realization.

ABOUT THE AUTHORS

Pete Barry is a playwright, screenwriter, actor, director and musician. Along with *Drop*, his short plays *Nine Point Eight Meters Per Second Per Second* and *The Banderscott* have been selected for performance in the Samuel French Off-Off Broadway Festival. His screenplay *10 Crimes in 2 Hours* was a finalist in the 13th Annual Writers Network Screenplay and Fiction Competition.

He is a cofounder of the Porch Room, a theater and film production company. He has produced and directed several collections of short plays, including *Five Cornered Thinking* at the New York Comedy Club and *Burt Reynolds Amazing Napalm Powered Oven and Other Paid Programming* in the 2001 New York Fringe Festival. A collection including four of his short plays, *Accidents Happen*, won the 2009 NJACT Perry Award for Outstanding Production of an Original Play.

Pete lives in the Lehigh Valley in Pennsylvania with his wife Jean and his daughter Lia.

J. Michael DeAngelis is a writer, actor and director. In addition to *Drop*, he has written or co-written the plays *Reunion Special, Reverie* and *Death in the Saloon*. He is one of the authors of and co-conceived *Accidents Happen*, which won the 2009 NJACT Perry Award for Outstanding Production of an Original Play. He starred in and co-wrote the short film *Tails Between Their Legs*, which was a winner of the National Film Challenge. *And God Spoke...*, a comedy pilot he wrote and directed, aired on SETV in Pennsylvania.

He is the Managing Director of the Porch Room, a collaborative theater and film production company, where he has written and performed in *An Evening on the Porch, Accidents Happen* and the short film, *Early Morning in the Tenement.*

A proud graduate of Muhlenberg College, Michael is an active performer-director with The Underground Shakespeare Company in Philadelphia, where he currently resides.

(Darkness. Clacking noises.)

MIKE. Can I tell you a secret?

RIC. Do I have a choice?

MIKE. I'm afraid of heights.

(A screeching noise, metal on metal. Short silence.)

RIC. You picked the perfect time to tell me.

(Lights up. RIC and MIKE, in the front car of a roller coaster. The coaster has stopped just before the largest dip.)

MIKE. Well. How high up do you suppose we are?

RIC. Oh, I was never really very good with large distances. We're high enough.

MIKE. I agree.

RIC. Are you all right?

MIKE. I really don't think so.

RIC. It's going to be fine. This kind of thing happens all the time.

MIKE. Oh my God, those things are people. Those walking raisins down there are people.

RIC. I wish I had a book.

MIKE. How long will it take them to start the ride, you think? No, don't tell me. Maybe we can just get down somehow.

RIC. There's no service ramp. Unless you want to unbuckle and climb back through the train, we're staying right here.

MIKE. UNBUCKLE? Are you insane? Unbuckle?

RIC. Just calm down. It'll start up again any minute.

MIKE. Don't say that!

RIC. Don't you want to get this over with?

MIKE. Ric, you are really not helping.

RIC. Hold on. So now, thanks to your dickwad cousin Brooke, I'm forced to actually live out my eight-year-old nightmare. You're yelling at Brooke to open the door, I just looked up at that head and I pissed in my G.I. Joe Underoos. I sat down in a puddle of urine and I cried myself into oblivion. Your dad came to get us out, what, ten minutes later? It might as well have been the entire Vietnam War. Still, when I came to, what happened? Your dad got me a change of clothes, got us some tall glasses of lemonade, and got your cousin Brooke grounded. Now, the moral of that twisted little anecdote is?

MIKE. Always wear clean Underoos?

RIC. I survived. There was no real danger. It was all in my mind. I didn't die in that garage, and I'm not going to die on this roller coaster.

MIKE. Ric. I think a two hundred foot fall is about seven billion times more likely to kill us than a stuffed deer's head. *(looking out over the side of the car)* Oh God, I'm making myself sick.

RIC. I told you, stop looking down. Look out there.

MIKE. That makes me nauseous. I'll just look at my feet. Oh, that makes me more nauseous.

RIC. How about craning your head around, look back at the rest of the train.

MIKE. You think that'll help?

RIC. Can't hurt.

MIKE. I guess you're right. *(He turns around.)* What's the worst it could be – OH MY GOD!

RIC. What?

MIKE. Holy shit! HOLY SHIT!

RIC. *(He turns around to look.)* Holy sweet potato pie.

MIKE. This is not happening. This is not happening.

RIC. *(calls offstage)* Hello? Can we help you?

JACKSON *(off)* Nope doing fine. Thanks.

RIC. Sure thing. *(beat)* You know, I can't help but notice you're scaling the scaffolding. Would you consider climbing on top of the tracks rather than underneath them?

JACKSON *(off)* Nah, I couldn't find the problem then.

RIC. Oh, I see. *(to MIKE)* It's OK, Mike, it's just the engineer. He's fixing the train.

MIKE. FIXING THE TRAIN? I can point my TV remote at my garage door and it will open from five hundred feet away. You're telling me they can't start an electric train by remote? WHAT CENTURY ARE WE IN THAT THESE MACEDONIANS MUST SEND A MAN TO CERTAIN DISMEMBERMENT SIMPLY TO FIX A MECHANICAL GLITCH?

RIC. Here he comes.

MIKE. Oh please God no.

*(**JACKSON** clambers over to them. He crawls all over the scaffolding, completely unafraid, looking for the problem.)*

JACKSON. Hiya boys.

RIC. Shouldn't you be wearing a safety harness or something?

JACKSON. Nah. They chafe me.

MIKE. Holy God.

RIC. That's very interesting. Have you found the problem?

JACKSON. Well, it's definitely this cart.

MIKE. Holy God.

RIC. Excuse my friend. He's a little shaken up.

JACKSON. Oh, yeah? Don't you worry, buddy. We'll zoom you straight to the ground.

MIKE. Holy God.

RIC. What do you think it is?

JACKSON. Eh. Never know. Something caught on the axle, electrical failure. Sometimes junk gets on the tracks. That's bad. I've seen carts derailed because of that, they flip up in the air, hundreds of feet sometimes.

MIKE. Holy God. Holy God.

RIC. Sounds great.

JACKSON. It's quite a spectacle, actually.

(*JACKSON suddenly howls in pain and pulls both hands away from the train, holding himself up by the sheer strength of his legs.*)

MIKE. WHAT WHAT?!?

JACKSON. *(nursing his hand)* Damn. That hurt.

MIKE. Perhaps you could put your hands back on the roller coaster.

RIC. What the hell's the matter with you?

MIKE. PERHAPS YOU COULD PUT YOUR HANDS BACK ON THE ROLLER COASTER.

JACKSON. Hey, buddy.

MIKE. KEEP YOUR HANDS AND ARMS INSIDE THE VEHICLE AT ALL TIMES, ISN'T THAT WHAT THEY TELL YOU?

JACKSON. Hey, buddy, look.

(*He puts his hands back on the train.*)

MIKE. Thank you. Thank you. I'm sorry. I'm sorry, I'm having a bad day.

RIC. He's just afraid of heights. Oh, I'm sorry – he's just afraid of dying.

JACKSON. Why? You got to go some time.

RIC. That's not the point. Look, could you just kind of reassure him that this ride is completely safe?

JACKSON. Safe? You kidding me? You'd never catch me on one these things.

MIKE. I'm gonna throw up.

RIC. OH NO YOU'RE NOT. Mike. Nobody is going to die, okay? I don't understand why you're so worked up about this all of a sudden.

MIKE. I told you, it's not all of a sudden. It's this secret I've kept with me for years. A very real and devastating fear of death.

MIKE. I don't know.

JACKSON. Wasn't as bad as you thought, was it? It was worse. Ha. Don't give up, buddy. Soon as this ride is over, get right back on and ride it again.

RIC. That's exactly what we're going to do. Are you almost finished?

JACKSON. Pretty much. This thing ain't very well put together at all. Whoops.

RIC. What do you mean, whoops?

JACKSON. This whole thing is pretty unstable.

RIC. Are you finished?

JACKSON. Yeah, I don't think I can do any more damage here.

RIC. Did anyone ever tell you that you have a sick sense of humor?

JACKSON. All the time. But I still can't do any more damage here. This thing's fucked.

RIC. Please say you're joking.

JACKSON. It'll drop though. Should go any minute.

(He prepares to leave.)

MIKE. Oh, good work.

JACKSON. Thank you.

RIC. Wait a minute. Where are you going? Don't you leave us if this train's not one hundred percent.

JACKSON. Have to, buddy. Power's coming on, don't wanna get cooked.

RIC. How can it run if it's "fucked"?

JACKSON. *(obviously)* Gravity.

RIC. WAIT! You stay right here and fix this train, or when we get to the ground, I'll have you fired!

JACKSON. You can't have me fired. I don't even work here.

(He leaves.)

RIC. WHAT?

MIKE. This is it.

RIC. HEY GET THE HELL BACK HERE!

MIKE. It's happening, Ric.

RIC. Oh my God we're gonna die.

MIKE. It's all right, Ric. I'm ready to do this.

RIC. I'M NOT.

MIKE. Just relax.

RIC. Mike, can I tell you a secret?

(Blackout. In the darkness, the sound of the roller coaster dropping. RIC screams in terror. MIKE howls in triumph.)

THE EDUCATION OF MACOLOCO

by Jen Silverman

THE EDUCATION OF MACOLOCO was first produced by the FUSION Theatre Company (FUSIONabq.org) as a winning entry in their annual original short works festival, The Seven, June 19th-22nd, 2008 at The Cell Theatre in Albuquerque, NM. Festival Producer: Dennis Gromelski. Festival Curator: Jen Grigg. Directed by Jen Grigg. Lighting and Scenic Design by Richard Hogle. Sound Design by Brent Stevens. Production Stage Manager: Maria Lee Schmidt. The cast was as follows:

MACOLOCO . . . . .Boris Plamenov Atanassov

ANESSA. . . . . Laurie Thomas

FATHER/NURSE. . . . . Bruce Holmes

THE EDUCATION OF MACOLOCO was also produced by the FUSION Theatre Company at the 34th Annual Samuel French OOB Festival at the Playwrights Horizons Theatre in NYC. Producer: Dennis Gromelski. Director: Jen Grigg. Lighting and Scenic Design: Richard Hogle. Sound Design: Brent Stevens. Production Stage Manager: Jacqueline Reid. The cast was as follows:

MACOLOCO. . . . . Ross Kelly

ANESSA . . . . .Laurie Thomas

FATHER/NURSE . . . . .Bruce Holmes

THE EDUCATION OF MACOLOCO has also been produced by Circus Theatricals in LA and LiveGirls! Theater in Seattle.

CHARACTERS

MACOLOCO
ANESSA
MACOLOCO'S FATHER / THE NURSE

TIME

Fluid

SET

The play seems to work best when the set is as minimal as possible.

PLAYWRIGHT'S NOTES

The jokes aren't mine, but I wish they were.

In the last scene of the play, the FUSION Theatre premiere projected writing over the stage, the actors, and the audience. This isn't necessary, but I loved it.

ABOUT THE AUTHOR

Jen Silverman is an MFA candidate at the University of Iowa Playwrights Workshop, scheduled to graduate in 2011. She received her BA from Brown University in 2006. Her plays include: *Lizardskin*, developed with New Georges in NYC, New York Stage & Film/ Powerhouse Theatre Company at Vassar College, and produced in the NYC International Fringe Festival in 2006; *The Education of Macoloco*, produced by FUSION Theatre Company in New Mexico, LiveGirls! in Seattle, Circus Theatricals in LA, and a 2009 winner of the Samuel French Off-Off Broadway Play Festival; *Crane Story*, developed with New Georges, the Bay Area Playwrights Festival in San Francisco, 2009 HotINK International Festival in NYC, and The Playwrights Realm in NYC; and *Nila*, which received its first workshop at The Lark's Playwrights Week 2009. Her plays *Akarui* and *Yellow City* have received workshop productions at the University of Iowa. Jen was a 2009 playwright in residence at the Hedgebrook International Women's Writers Residency.

(**MACOLOCO** *walks out. He navigates the stage like a minefield.*)

MACOLOCO. Twenty-seven years ago my mother gave birth to me. She was twelve years older than I am now. The hospital smelled like Drain-O and Jell-O. She was all alone except for the nurse, who smelled like Drain-O and Jell-O and vodka. My father called my mother from Georgia two hours and seventeen minutes after I was born, and they named me Colloquy. A colloquy is a talking together and that is what they did not do often enough. Forty-six hours after I was born, during their fifth and final phone call, my father decided he did not want to talk together anymore. Ever. And my name changed.

(beat)

These are the facts...and the facts are undeniable.

(deep breath)

You are about to see me being educated at the age of eight.

(**ANESSA** *enters. She is his mother. She navigates the stage like she is a landmine and she is looking for the best location to detonate. She Takes No Prisoners.*)

ANESSA. Macoloco! It is Time to be Educated! Pop Quiz:

(**MACOLOCO** *squares his shoulders. Very rapid:*)

ANESSA. There are how many breeds of penguins?
MACOLOCO. Seventeen!
ANESSA. The only animal that cannot jump is an –
MACOLOCO. Elephant!
ANESSA. The average pig has an orgasm for –
MACOLOCO. Thirty minutes!

ANESSA. *(sternly)* Are you sure?

MACOLOCO. Yes!

ANESSA. Are you sure?

MACOLOCO. *(less sure)* Yes...?

ANESSA. *(severe)* How do you know the pig is having an orgasm? How do you know that it is not the average copulation time of two pigs that is thirty minutes?

(**MACOLOCO** *is crushed.*)

ANESSA. Sex does not imply orgasm. Learn this, son.

(**MACOLOCO** *learns it. Quiz time resumes: fast and furious.*)

ANESSA. The only animal besides humans that can get leprosy is:

MACOLOCO. The armadillo!

ANESSA. The Sanskrit word for "war" means:

MACOLOCO. "Desire for more cows"!

ANESSA. How many pounds of force does it take to detach a human ear?

(*Beat.* **MACOLOCO** *doesn't know.*)

ANESSA. Well?

MACOLOCO. Idontknow.

ANESSA. Speak up! – and E.Nun.Ci.Ate.

MACOLOCO. I. Don't. Know.

ANESSA. You must always enunciate, son. And you must always readily admit to your shortcomings. Politicians don't do this and that is why we assassinate them. Do you want to be assassinated?

MACOLOCO. No.

ANESSA. Can you spell "Assassination"?

MACOLOCO. A-s-s-a-s-s-i-n-a-t-i-o-n.

ANESSA. Very good. And to return to the original question, it takes seven pounds of force to detach a human ear. Say it after me.

MACOLOCO. Seven pounds.

ANESSA. Take a deep breath.

(They take a deep breath together)

What are these called?

MACOLOCO. *(excited, he knows this)* The facts!

ANESSA. Don't yell.

MACOLOCO. *(quieter)* They are the facts.

ANESSA. Exactly. And the facts are undeniable.

(ANESSA walks over to the chair and sits down. She sits like she is conquering a small country. MACOLOCO turns his back on her, and speaks to us.)

MACOLOCO. I was educated at home. That is to say: It is at home that I learned to deal with the Facts. It is Crucial that one learns to deal with Facts. When nuclear fallout blinds us and the sun grows dim, the only weapons we have will be the Facts and our ability to deal with them. The pragmatists will survive and repopulate the planet. That is what my mother says. You are about to see me being educated at the age of thirteen.

ANESSA. Macoloco.

It is Time to be Educated!

(She stands. MACOLOCO snaps to attention. She walks the ranks of an army of one.)

ANESSA. You are becoming a man, Macoloco. Inexorably. Unpreventably. And it is my duty to tell you what this entails.

Chin up. Eyes forward.

What you have to look forward to: genital development, pubic hair, a general growth spurt, a series of mildly enjoyable and meaningless ejaculations, followed by a voice change.

(MACOLOCO raises his hand tentatively.)

I will answer any questions after the lesson. Put your hand down.

A man will ejaculate approximately eighteen quarts of semen in his lifetime. Men are six times more likely than women to peruse sexually explicit material on the Internet. At age seventy, seventy-three percent of men are still potent. Half of the men raised on farms have had a sexual encounter with an animal. Odors that increase blood flow to the penis are: lavender, licorice, eucalyptus, pomegranate, and pumpkin pie.

(MACOLOCO raises his hand again.)

ANESSA. *(cont.)* Save your questions until the end. Hand down. Shoulders squared.

One may assume that at some point in your life you will enter into a sexual partnership with a woman. This partnership cannot be expected to last long, and most promises made within its confines will soon be rendered null and void. However, on the offchance that you still wish to pursue such an encounter, I will teach you about women. Women with a Ph.D. are twice as likely to be interested in a one-night stand than those with only an undergraduate degree. Women blink twice as much as men. It has been estimated that one out of every two hundred women is born with an extra nipple. These are the facts and the facts are?

MACOLOCO. Undeniable.

ANESSA. Precisely. Now I will take questions.

MACOLOCO. Who was my dad?

(Beat. ANESSA is thrown off.)

ANESSA. That is an entirely different topic.

MACOLOCO. What was his name? Where is he?

ANESSA. That is unrelated to the current subject of your education.

MACOLOCO. Mom?

ANESSA. Class is over for the day. You may go outside.

(She walks away from him and sits in the chair. He turns to us.)

MACOLOCO. *(dryly)* It was what one might call a specialized education. As I was a self-motivated child, I engaged in a great number of independent studies. That is to say, I independently studied the contents of my mother's desk and file cabinets when she was out. May I present: Exhibit A.

(He takes out an envelope.)

MACOLOCO. *(cont.)* Found in her sock drawer, inside a sturdy wool sock.

(He takes the letter out of the envelope but doesn't read it. Enter Macoloco's **FATHER**. *He has an outrageous German accent.)*

FATHER. My dearest Anessa: I haf had a dream of you again. Togezzer ve are standink on a great dune of sand, we are holdink hands und ze ocean is rollink beneath us und ze wafes are thunderous – und zen I feel zer is a tension in your hand, I turn to you, you are shoutink but I cannot hear your vords. Und zo I shout back: VAAAAAT? Your eyes are vide, you are panicking und so am I, and ve are screamink back and fors at each other but ve cannot hear...

(His voice dies away.)

MACOLOCO. Perhaps it was my over-exposure to Rilke as a child, but the dark silences and furrowed brow evoked in my mother by the mere mention of my father made me feel that he must be German. Yet, as a teenager, I entertained the possibility that he might be French. See Exhibit B.

(another letter)

Found in her underwear drawer, at the bottom of the pile.

FATHER. *(outrageous French accent)* My dearest Anessa: Today ze sea is so bright and ze air is warm and I have decideed to become a paintair. I will paint your portrait from every picture of you in my possession, yet none of zem will be as beautiful as the original.

MACOLOCO. *(a flicker of doubt)* He couldn't have been Russian…?

FATHER. *(outrageous Russian accent)* My dearest Anessa: Although I am six times more likely than you to peruse explicit material on the Internet, I am dewoted to you. At age seventy, I vill be among sewenty-three percent of men still potent, and –

MACOLOCO. Enough!

*(Russian **FATHER** falls silent.)*

My father is the subject of much conjecture but very few facts. As for his letters, I only ever found three. And they were very short. May I present: the first.

*(He opens the first but before he can read it, **ANESSA** calls him:)*

ANESSA. Macoloco!

MACOLOCO. Just a minute!

(to us)

Exhibit A –

ANESSA. Macoloco!

MACOLOCO. I'm coming!

ANESSA. Son!!

MACOLOCO. *(puts the letters away)* But that is an entirely different topic. Let us proceed. You are about to see me being educated at the age of twenty-five: two years and three months prior to today.

*(**ANESSA** approaches him. She carries herself differently. Old. Worn thin.)*

ANESSA. Son.

MACOLOCO. Yes, mother.

ANESSA. Sit down.

*(He hesitates. She gestures, impatient. Uncertainly, **MACOLOCO** sits down in the chair.)*

ANESSA. Pop-quiz. What is the most common form of dementia?

MACOLOCO. I don't know.

ANESSA. Hint: it is an incurable, progressive degenerative disease of the brain.

MACOLOCO. Schizophrenia?

ANESSA. Hint: it is named after Dr. Alois Alzheimer.

MACOLOCO. Um. Alzheimers?

ANESSA. Bingo.

(*beat*)

MACOLOCO. …Mother?

(**ANESSA** *is exhausted all of a sudden.* **MACOLOCO** *jumps up. He seats her in the chair.*)

MACOLOCO. Mother.

ANESSA. I wasn't going to tell you.

MACOLOCO. Mom!…

ANESSA. It became necessary.

MACOLOCO. I don't understand.

ANESSA. Don't be ridiculous, of course you do. You have a solid grounding in all of the facts you will need. The majority, shall I say, of the facts that you –

(*Her attention is wandering, she stares at her hands.*)

MACOLOCO. …Mom?

(*A long beat. She shakes herself out of it. She doesn't quite remember what they were talking about, but she remembers that she has to tell him something.*)

ANESSA. What were we – ? Ah. Son. I was looking for you. Pop-quiz. What is the most common form of – ?

(*The word eludes her.*)

The most common form of –

MACOLOCO. It's called Alzheimer's.

ANESSA. (*distant*) Ah. Yes. I think so too.

(**MACOLOCO** *leaves her in the chair. Back to us.*)

MACOLOCO. It's called Alzheimer's.

(beat)

MACOLOCO. *(cont.)* As a child, I was educated at home. As an adult, I began to realize precisely where the holes in my education lay. For example: how does one talk to the progressively ill? And what does one bring them?

*(He crosses to **ANESSA** in the chair. Visiting hours. He carries flowers.)*

MACOLOCO. I brought you flowers.

ANESSA. What have I said to you about flowers.

MACOLOCO. Tulip bulbs can be used in place of onions for cooking?

ANESSA. Where did you learn that?

MACOLOCO. *(gently)* From you.

ANESSA. Oh. Well. No, I meant that I don't like flowers. They're unnecessary.

(beat)

MACOLOCO. How do you feel? The nurses said you've been doing better.

ANESSA. I'm fine, Mac. I've been telling you that I'm fine. He's a healthy, seven pound baby boy.

MACOLOCO. …Mother?

ANESSA. We should name him something distinctive. Columbus, perhaps. Yet there's the problem of all those oppressed native peoples. Perhaps Columbus is not the best name.

MACOLOCO. It's me. It's Macoloco.

ANESSA. I know you wanted Mac Jr. But that's so…plebeian.

MACOLOCO. Mother, come back.

ANESSA. It means "commonplace."

(flicker of doubt)

I think. Commonwealth? No. Common. I don't want our son to be common.

MACOLOCO. *(away, to us)* "Mac." It's not a very German name…or French. Or Russian.

(lying to himself)

Mac-chievelli?

(*Macoloco's* **FATHER** *walks on, agreeably.*)

FATHER. (*outrageous Italian accent*) Ay! Mi amor! You have given me a healthy eight pound bambino! Mi bellissima Anessa!

MACOLOCO. Shut up.

(*Macoloco's* **FATHER** *blinks, a little surprised, but shuts up.*)

MACOLOCO. Why does she want to talk to you? You're twenty-seven years in the past tense. You left her. You didn't love her. You're not even European. Why you?

(*His* **FATHER** *shrugs, hands spread: who knows?*)

Fuck.

(**MACOLOCO** *turns away. When he turns back to us, it is with dignity born of desperation. He takes out the letters, one after the other.*)

How to lie is as much a part of any child's education as how to tell the truth. You are about to hear the truth. Of the three letters which I found, the first two are from my mother. Only the third is from my father. May I present: Exhibit A, Letter One.

(**ANESSA**, *center-stage. Young* **ANESSA**, *self-contained but not cold. Wistful.*)

ANESSA. Dear Mac, I liked your joke. Here's a better one: How many mice does it take to screw in a light-bulb?

(*beat*)

Only two, but I don't know how they get in. Also, I miss you. Did you buy the ticket yet? I'll meet you at the airport. Love, Anessa.

MACOLOCO. Exhibit B, Letter Two:

ANESSA. Dear Mac, what do you mean you don't get it? It's a double-entendre employing the pivotal word "screw." Screw in. *Screw* in. I've drawn a diagram at the bottom of the page in case you're still having difficulty. Also, what do you mean "unforeseen problems"? If you don't buy a ticket now, you won't be here on time. He's due in a few weeks. Mac, I want you here. I need you to be here with me for this. Yours, Anessa.

MACOLOCO. *(to* **ANESSA***)* Jokes? You told each other jokes? Why didn't you ever tell me jokes?

(beat, tries to calm himself, another outburst)

He didn't even understand your jokes! I know what a double entendre is!

(beat, composes himself this time)

Exhibit C, Letter Three.

(beat)

I lied again. The third letter isn't from my father. It's from his mother. My grandmother.

ANESSA. *(takes out the third letter, reads)* Please stop sending mail, he ain't here no more, I don't know where he gone. Here's all the things you sent, they ain't been opened, please don't send them no more, yrs, Lucy.

*(***ANESSA** *drops the letter on the ground. Beat. She returns to her chair and becomes old again.* **MACOLOCO** *picks up the letter. He reads it to himself.)*

MACOLOCO. OK. If that's what you…

(defeated, resolute)

OK.

(He crosses over to **ANESSA** *in her chair. A jovial male* **NURSE** *intercepts* **MACOLOCO***.)*

NURSE. Hey there kid, how you doin' today.

MACOLOCO. Hey Freddy. I'm just here to see my mom. How're you?

NURSE. You know how it is, parkin' tickets and coffee stains – hey, uh, this is the thing though, your mom, today's one of her days.

MACOLOCO. Did she break all the plates again? Or something more expensive?

NURSE. She's thinkin' we got the whole place bugged, she's thinkin' she's a spy. This morning she had herself convinced this was North Korea.

MACOLOCO. And now?

NURSE. Now it's Guantanamo.

(The **NURSE** *shows* **MACOLOCO** *to the chair.* **ANESSA** *is crouched behind it.)*

ANESSA. Shhh-hhhh-hhhh! They've got a voice-lock in effect! Get down!

MACOLOCO. *(crouches down next to her)* A voice-lock?

ANESSA. If they can get a lock on your voice, they'll beam you up!
Who're you?

MACOLOCO. I'm Mac.

*(***ANESSA** *looks at him. She almost knows that name.)*

ANESSA. Do I know you?

MACOLOCO. Yeah. You write me letters. We tell each other jokes but I don't get yours.

ANESSA. *(this rings a bell)* I bet you haven't bought the ticket.

MACOLOCO. No, I did.

ANESSA. Really?

MACOLOCO. Really. I'll be there.

ANESSA. Because he's due any day now.

MACOLOCO. I can't wait.

ANESSA. *(shy)* Oh. OK.

MACOLOCO. Want to hear a joke while we're waiting?
How many mice does it take to screw in a light-bulb?

ANESSA. What kind of a joke is that?

MACOLOCO. Two, but I don't know how they got in there.
It's a double-entendre.

*(***ANESSA** *laughs. We can see shades of Young* **ANESSA**. **MACOLOCO** *stares at her, stunned.)*

ANESSA. I get it. It's a good joke.
What?

MACOLOCO. I've never seen you laugh.

ANESSA. I can appreciate a good joke.

MACOLOCO. Want to hear another? What's a transistor?

(She doesn't know.)

Want to guess?

ANESSA. *(smiles)* I'm sleepy, Mac, just tell me.

MACOLOCO. A priest in nun's clothes.

ANESSA. That's another double-entendre, isn't it. I don't remember you being quite so good at those.

MACOLOCO. I've improved. Why do so many blondes move to LA?

…It's easy to spell.

ANESSA. That's silly.

(She yawns.)

I'm tired now, Mac. You should go. I can't get tired before the baby comes.

(She turns away from him.)

MACOLOCO. *(grasping)* Just one more. Anessa? Are you still there? Mom?

ANESSA. Bring me paper.

MACOLOCO. *(can't pretend anymore)* Mom, it's me now. It's not Mac anymore.

ANESSA. I want to write a letter.

*(**MACOLOCO** takes the paper wrapped around the flowers, and gives her a pen. She starts to write, slowly, painstakingly.)*

MACOLOCO. Who are you writing to, Mom?

(She doesn't answer him.)

Mom?

*(The lights down on **MACOLOCO** kneeling by his mother, watching her write. One light up on **ANESSA**. She sits alone. She has written all over everything. Words spiral and sprawl over the whole stage. She tries to begin.)*

ANESSA. Dear son.

> *(starts again)*

ANESSA. *(cont.)* Dear…Macoloco.

> *(struggling)*
>
> I have always –
> you have been – for me, you have always been –
> and as I have watched you grow – I have –
> I –
> I have felt –
>
> *(But there is no way. There's no way. She's never learned how to say this.)*

ANESSA. It is time now to be educated by others. It is time to be educated.

> *(Lights down on* ANESSA, *crumpled pages in her hand, all of it unspoken.)*

End of Play

realer than that

by Kitt Lavoie

realer than that was developed with the CRY HAVOC Workshop (www.cryhavoccompany.org).

realer than that was first produced by the Sounding Theatre Company, *"Sound Bytes" One-Act Festival,* Abingdon Theatre Arts Complex, May 28, 2005-June 8, 2005. Directed by Jocelyn Sawyer. The cast was as follows:

JARED...Chris Flynn
COLLEEN ....Noelle Holly

realer than that also ran at the Manhattan Repertory Theatre, 2006 Fall One-Act Play Festival, Manhattan Repertory Theatre, October 11, 2006-October 14, 2006. Directed by Kitt Lavoie. The cast was as follows:

JARED..Russell Hankin
COLLEEN ....Jenny Kirlin

realer than that was performed by The CRY HAVOC Company at the The 34th Annual Samuel French Off Off Broadway Short Play Festival, Playwrights Horizons Mainstage Theater, July 18, 2009-July 19, 2009. Directed by Kitt Lavoie, with Jenny Kirlin as Associate Director. The cast was as follows:

JARED..Josh Bywater
COLLEEN ....Aubyn Philabaum

CHARACTERS

Jared – A young man, 26
Colleen – A young woman, also 26

ABOUT THE AUTHOR

Kitt Lavoie is author of twenty-one produced plays and musical books, including *Twice Rather Perish*, *The Median Line* (both winners of the Herbert J. Robinson Award for Dramatic Writing), *realer than that* (winner, Samuel French OOB Festival), *[pwnd]* (NYIT Award Nominee, Best Original Short Script), and the widely-produced *Good Enough* and *Party Girl*. He has directed more than eighty productions in New York City, including the original productions of more than thirty plays, and recently made his film writing/directing debut with *Rainbow Rabbit Reliant*. Also an acting coach and teacher, his students currently appear on Broadway, Off-Broadway, on television, and in major films. Kitt holds a Master of Fine Arts in Directing from the Actors Studio Drama School and is a Member of the Stage Directors and Choreographers Society and Artistic Director of The CRY HAVOC Company, which focuses on developing new plays (www.cryhavoccompany.org). Visit www.kittlavoie.com for more information.

(Lights rise on an economy hotel room. The room is dark. After a moment, keys jangle in the hallway. The door swings open. **COLLEEN,** *26, in a dressy pair of pants and blouse, enters, followed quickly by* **JARED,** *also 26, in a suit. As soon as* **JARED** *shuts the door,* **COLLEEN** *pounces on him, kissing him hard and pushing him up against the door, unbuttoning her shirt as she does. After a moment, she digs into her purse, pulling out a condom. She puts the wrapped condom between her teeth and slides down the front of* **JARED** *onto her knees, going forcefully for his belt. She undoes the belt, then reaches for his pants button. With a quick move,* **JARED** *slips out from between* **COLLEEN** *and the door, leaving her on her knees.)*

JARED. Hey. Let's just…

*(***JARED*** goes to the light switch and flips on the light.* **COLLEEN** *gets up and moves for* **JARED.** *He sidesteps her.)*

JARED. It's good to see you. How have you been?

COLLEEN. Fine.

*(***COLLEEN*** goes to the bed and slides out of her pants, hanging them over a chair.)*

JARED. We don't have to do this.

COLLEEN. I want to.

JARED. I've missed you.

*(***COLLEEN*** slides onto the bed.)*

JARED. Do you want anything?

COLLEEN. Not really.

JARED. A coke or something?

COLLEEN. What have you got?

JARED. Nothing. I mean, I can go down the hall to the machine.

COLLEEN. That's okay.

JARED. Water?

COLLEEN. Fine.

JARED. I *have* missed you.

(**JARED** *goes into the bathroom. Water runs. He returns with two glasses of water, bringing one to* **COLLEEN.**)

JARED. You miss me?

COLLEEN. It's been nine years.

JARED. Yeah. Do you?

COLLEEN. What does that mean, "you miss me"?

JARED. I think about you.

COLLEEN. And what does that mean?

JARED. I wonder what you're doing. And think about... stuff. We did. And...I just *think* about you. You never think about me?

COLLEEN. You occur to me.

JARED. Well...maybe that's what I mean, then. I don't know. I loved you. And so I think about you. From time to time. And I hope that you're happy. Are you happy?

COLLEEN. I'm fine.

JARED. I *do* think about you. I'm not going to apologize for that. You were my first. First love. My first...Jesus. *(a beat)* I didn't know you were going to be there tonight. It was good to see you.

COLLEEN. You, too.

JARED. I bet. After I'd "occurred" to you so often.

COLLEEN. There's no need to be so...fucking...*hurt* about it.

JARED. Did you love me?

(No response.)

JARED. You said you did is all.

COLLEEN. I was seventeen.

JARED. So?

COLLEEN. So I loved you seventeen. I don't know if that's the same thing.

JARED. I think it is.

(COLLEEN gulps down the end of her water, slamming the glass onto the nightstand. She pulls off her shirt, tossing it onto the chair with her pants.)

COLLEEN. Let's go.

(COLLEEN crawls down the bed towards JARED. He backs away.)

JARED. Why did you come back here?

COLLEEN. What do you mean?

JARED. Why did you come back here? Tonight?

COLLEEN. It was a wedding. It's what you do after a wedding.

JARED. So you're just looking to get laid?

COLLEEN. Why, you looking for a commitment?

JARED. No, I'm just saying...

COLLEEN. I'm a big girl.

JARED. Yeah, I guess.

COLLEEN. Yeah.

JARED. It was just so much work to get in your pants the first time. I think I'm just thrown by the lack of challenge.

COLLEEN. Yeah. So, you ready?

(a beat)

JARED. I really have missed you.

COLLEEN. What do you want?

JARED. I want to do it right. When we did it, we didn't do it right. It was all graduation and get it in and say we did it and...I mean, I wanted to make love to you. That's what I mean, when I think about you. That, and just how you're doing. But we never made love. Really. And I think about that I wish that we did. Because it would have been right.

COLLEEN. Right?

JARED. Yeah. And, you know – why not do it now? The way we should have done it. Not under the bleachers, but in a bed. And with...*Right*, you know? I know it's stupid. But I think about it a lot.

COLLEEN. Look, Jared, if you don't want to fuck me...I can't do this romantic.

JARED. When you came back for the Fourth after freshman year, I wanted to tell you. *That's* why I wrote to you. Because I wanted to talk, when you came home. To fix it. And I wanted to...do it *right*. Then. On the beach. With the sky lit up. I had it all planned. And you showed up with what's-his-name.

COLLEEN. Ted.

JARED. Ted, yeah. Wouldn't that have been great, though? Water lapping, your face lit up and looking at me.

(**COLLEEN** *reaches to pull off her undershirt.*)

COLLEEN. Come on.

JARED. Did you make love to *him*? That weekend?

(**COLLEEN** *lets go of her undershirt.*)

COLLEEN. No.

JARED. Ever?

COLLEEN. Yeah.

JARED. Like, real love?

COLLEEN. I married him. Two months after graduation.

JARED. Oh. *(a beat)* I'm sorry. What happened?

COLLEEN. Nothing.

(a beat)

JARED. You're still...

COLLEEN. Yeah. Like I said, I can't do this romantic. So let's fuck.

(**COLLEEN** *slides down the bed towards* **JARED**. *He gets up from the chair and moves away.*)

JARED. I'm not sure that this...is a good idea.

COLLEEN. It matters?

JARED. Yes.

COLLEEN. To you?

JARED. Yes.

COLLEEN. That I'm married?

*(**JARED** just looks at her.)*

COLLEEN. I'm surprised.

JARED. You shouldn't be.

COLLEEN. It didn't seem to matter that Jannelle was married.

*(A small smile crosses **JARED**'s face.)*

JARED. You watched it?

COLLEEN. Night vision doesn't lie.

JARED. No, but Fox editors do. Nothing actually happened. They were just trying to sex it up.

COLLEEN. Seemed to work out pretty well for you.

JARED. I guess. But you watched?

COLLEEN. How could I not?

JARED. *(holding his fingers an inch apart) This* close.

COLLEEN. What do you do, right?

JARED. I got twenty-five thousand. Not half a mil, but…

COLLEEN. I want you to fuck me, Jared.

JARED. You really watched?

*(**COLLEEN** nods.)*

COLLEEN. Come on.

JARED. You vote for me?

COLLEEN. I don't do that kind of thing.

*(**COLLEEN** and **JARED** look at each other for a moment. He walks to the edge of the bed, leans in, and kisses her gently. She kisses him back, harder. She climbs atop him and continues to kiss him aggressively as she begins to undress him. She digs into his chest with her nails. He begins kissing her harder, reaching up and grabbing her by the back of the neck to pull her closer. She jerks suddenly away. He stops.)*

JARED. *(gently)* We really don't have to.

COLLEEN. I said I want to.

> (**COLLEEN** *leans suddenly into* **JARED** *and begins kissing him – hard. She grabs his hand and places it on her breast. She rolls him over so that he is on top of her. They continue to kiss as she continues to hold his hand on her breast. After a moment, he pulls away, yanks his hand from her grip, and kneels over her. They look at each other.)*

COLLEEN. Come on…

> (*She reaches for his crotch. He gently moves her hands away.*)

JARED. Did you see it?

> (*She begins to sit up to kiss him. He moves aside.*)

JARED. Did you?

COLLEEN. Yeah. Come on…

> (**COLLEEN** *sits up and kisses* **JARED** *hard. He pulls immediately away, moving to the other side of the bed.*)

JARED. I'm just saying, I told you I think about you.

COLLEEN. Will you just *fuck* me. For real, Jared. Come on.

> (**COLLEEN** *sits up, lifts her T-shirt and grasps the waistband of her underwear, ready to pull them down.* **JARED** *grabs her hands firmly. She tries to pull her underwear down, but he prevents her. He pulls her hands from her side. She continues to struggle.*)

JARED. Come on. Can't this just be nice.

COLLEEN. I don't want it nice. I want you to *fuck* me.

JARED. Well, I don't want to.

> (**COLLEEN** *continues to struggle.* **JARED** *pushes her back on the bed.*)

JARED. *Jesus.*

> (**JARED** *looks down on* **COLLEEN**. *She looks back.*)

JARED. You're different than I remember.

COLLEEN. Fuck you.

> (**JARED** *sits at the table. He and* **COLLEEN** *stare at each other across the room.*)

COLLEEN. I can't do it like this, either.

JARED. If *you* could have dinner with anyone in the world, who would *it* be?

COLLEEN. Fuck you.

JARED. 'Cause I said you.

COLLEEN. I know.

JARED. They asked and I said you.

COLLEEN. I saw.

JARED. I thought that might mean something.

COLLEEN. Not really.

JARED. I mean, I thought maybe you didn't know. They bleeped it out.

COLLEEN. No, I could tell.

JARED. They bleeped it.

COLLEEN. I asked them to.

JARED. How?

COLLEEN. They called and asked permission to use my name. I said no.

JARED. Oh.

COLLEEN. *But you could tell.*

> (*silence*)

JARED. But doesn't that mean anything?

COLLEEN. Are we gonna fuck?

JARED. You still want to?

COLLEEN. Not really, but yeah.

JARED. Well…not like this.

> (*a beat*)

COLLEEN. Then I'm going.

> (**COLLEEN** *gets up and goes for her pants hung over the chair.* **JARED** *snatches them up and takes them to the other side of the room.*)

COLLEEN. Give them.

JARED. *It doesn't mean anything???*

COLLEEN. Give them to me!

JARED. Anything?

COLLEEN. Give me my fucking pants!

JARED. No.

> (**COLLEEN** *turns and goes to* **JARED**'s *suitcase, on the floor. She opens it up and takes out a pair of men's pants.* **JARED** *bounds over the bed and snatches them from her. He grabs the suitcase and drags it across the room.*)

COLLEEN. Give them back!

JARED. "If you could have dinner with anyone in the world, who would it be?"

COLLEEN. Give them!

JARED. "Colleen. My girlfriend from high school. 'Cause she was my first love and I want to know that she's happy."

COLLEEN. I'm sure all your little internet girl-fans fucking creamed themselves over that.

JARED. That's not what that was about.

COLLEEN. "Didja fuck 'er, Jared?"

JARED. That guy was a prick.

COLLEEN. "Didja?"

JARED. He was being a dick and I said, "I was with her."

COLLEEN. Fuck you!

JARED. "I was with her" was pretty diplomatic, I think.

COLLEEN. *Do* you?

JARED. I got twenty-five thousand dollars out of those two weeks, plus an astonishing number of unreally attractive women writing me these *filthy* e-mails, sidling up to me on the street. And I'm not used to that kind of thing, Colleen. I never have been. But the only thing I *ever* hoped after that episode aired was that I would hear from you again. These five weeks, every new e-mail, every ring of the phone, that's all I've wished. Doesn't that mean anything?

COLLEEN. Give me my pants.

JARED. Doesn't that mean *anything?*

COLLEEN. Yes.

JARED. What?

COLLEEN. Give me my pants!

JARED. What does it mean?

COLLEEN. It means my husband fucking watches reality TV, is what it means! Who'd've guessed? I wouldn't've. Now give me my fucking pants.

JARED. What does that mean?

COLLEEN. My fucking marriage is over, Jared. Almost ten years since I've seen you and you fucking ended my marriage.

JARED. How?

(a beat)

COLLEEN. I told him I was a virgin, Jared. When we met. That he was my first.

JARED. Why would – ?

COLLEEN. 'Cause I wanted him to be. 'Cause I wanted him to be and so I told him that he was. I was nineteen. I didn't think I'd end up *marrying* him. But you know what – after two, three…*seven* years, a little dorm room bunk-bed fantasy can begin to feel an awful lot like a lie.

JARED. Well, it is.

COLLEEN. Fuck you!

JARED. What? It's not supposed to matter to me? You were *my* first, Colleen. And I was yours.

COLLEEN. You weren't my *first.* Don't say that.

JARED. You said I was.

COLLEEN. Ted was. I wanted Ted to be and he would have been if you hadn't fucking told the world.

JARED. Why would you tell him that?

COLLEEN. 'Cause I wanted it to be true.

JARED. It don't make it so.

COLLEEN. I *wanted* it to be.

JARED. Why?

COLLEEN. 'Cause I didn't want to be who I was anymore. I wanted to be new.

JARED. New?

COLLEEN. He made me feel good, Jared. Not good, like, "happy." Good like a good person. And not dirty. I didn't want to be that girl anymore.

JARED. What girl?

COLLEEN. *I didn't want to be some girl that got raped anymore.*

(**JARED** *is taken aback. He looks at her a moment.*)

COLLEEN. So I started new like it didn't happen and it was fine.

JARED. I'm sorry.

COLLEEN. "Some girl." That's what it felt like for – …Then the fucking phone rings. "I saw your boyfriend on TV tonight, honey. Is there anything else you want to tell me?" "Yeah, I guess there are a couple things…"

(**JARED** *moves gently towards her.*)

JARED. Are you okay?

COLLEEN. Don't.

JARED. What?

COLLEEN. Don't look at me like that.

JARED. Like what?

COLLEEN. Like I need to be taken care of. That's how Ted looks now. All the time.

JARED. I thought you said he was leaving.

COLLEEN. No. *No.* He's been fucking *perfect.* Always taking care of me. Always *so* careful whenever we touch – on the rare occasion that we touch anymore – always so careful to be sure that he's making love to me.

JARED. That sounds –

COLLEEN. It's *always* making love now, Jared. He won't *fuck me* anymore.

JARED. Well –

COLLEEN. That's all I wanted from you tonight. I thought you could handle it.

(a beat)

JARED. I can't. Look, I have been looking forward to tonight for a long time. You have no idea. But it sounds like you've got a good guy. Ted –

COLLEEN. No –

JARED. And it sounds like he's willing to work through whatever –

COLLEEN. It's over, Jared.

JARED. It sounds like he can deal with what happened.

COLLEEN. That's *all* he does anymore. Is deal with it. And it makes something that felt like it had almost gone away really fucking hard to forget. All the time.

JARED. You didn't do anything wrong.

COLLEEN. *I know I didn't.* That's why I wanted to fuck you tonight. So I *would've* done something wrong. So it would be okay the way he treats me. And I wouldn't have to hate him.

JARED. You shouldn't hate him.

COLLEEN. Maybe not. But I do sometimes.

JARED. Sleeping with me wouldn't make it any better.

COLLEEN. It might.

JARED. It won't.

COLLEEN. It's all I think about, Jared. How I hate him. Nothing will change until that goes away.

(a beat)

JARED. I won't have sex with you, Colleen.

(a beat)

COLLEEN. I can't make you.

JARED. No.

COLLEEN. I'm going.

(**COLLEEN** *retrieves her pants. She sits on the edge of the bed and pulls them on. a beat*)

JARED. I am sorry.

COLLEEN. Yeah, you said.

JARED. I know.

(**COLLEEN** *scoops up her socks and shoes and begins to put them on.*)

JARED. Do you mind...?

COLLEEN. I'm sure I do.

JARED. I mean...I'm sorry...but what happened?

COLLEEN. What do you mean?

JARED. When you...I just feel awful that I didn't know. I would have done whatever, you know, to help. If I'd known...What...When did it happen? Who did it to you?

(**COLLEEN** *just looks at him.*)

I'm sorry. It's none of my business.

(**COLLEEN** *just looks at him.*)

What?

(**COLLEEN** *breaks eye contact and pulls on her shoes.*)

JARED. *What?*

COLLEEN. *You did it,* Jared.

JARED. Excuse me?

COLLEEN. I'm going.

(**COLLEEN** *moves for the door.* **JARED** *gets in her way.*)

JARED. *What does that mean?*

COLLEEN. You did it, Jared. *You* raped me.

JARED. I did not.

COLLEEN. You did.

JARED. We only had sex that one time.

COLLEEN. Yeah.

JARED. Fuck you, Colleen.

COLLEEN. You – …

JARED. What do you want?

COLLEEN. I should go.

JARED. No. What the fuck do you want from me?

COLLEEN. Nothing. I just want to go.

JARED. Out of the fucking woodwork people have been coming. But *this* –

COLLEEN. *I don't want anything from you.* I just wanted you to fuck me. And that was a stupid idea.

JARED. Yeah.

COLLEEN. Stupid. Fine. I'm going.

JARED. No. Not until you promise me you're not telling anybody this bullshit story.

COLLEEN. It's not a bullshit –

JARED. You're not going to get your fifteen minutes off my back like this.

COLLEEN. That's not what I'm doing.

JARED. Then what *are* you doing?

COLLEEN. I don't know.

JARED. *No one* will believe you, you know. You do realize that? Not after you came back here tonight. How would you explain that?

COLLEEN. I wouldn't –

JARED. For real, Colleen. If you thought I did to you what you say I did to you – why would you come back here with me?

COLLEEN. *This isn't about you, Jared.*

JARED. Then *why?*

COLLEEN. You wouldn't understand.

JARED. Then why *me?*

COLLEEN. Because you *owe* me.

(a beat)

COLLEEN. All you had to do was fuck me, Jared. That's all I wanted.

JARED. That's all you *ever* wanted.

COLLEEN. Why would I have wanted to fuck you under the goddamn *bleachers?*

JARED. You did.

COLLEEN. Believe me, Jared, I didn't.

JARED. You were giving me all the signs.

COLLEEN. I wasn't giving you *anything.*

JARED. You had my fucking cock in your mouth. What was I supposed to think?

COLLEEN. That you were getting a blowjob.

JARED. That's not funny.

COLLEEN. It's *not* funny. It cost me a lot. To decide to do that for you. You were leaving the next day, and I wanted to do something for you. And *look* what you turned it into.

(He stares at her.)

JARED. That was the best sex I ever had, Colleen. The one time that it actually felt like it meant something. And it means something to me. And look what *you're* turning it into.

(They stare at each other a moment.)

I was so mad at you that night, you know. That you didn't come out to the beach with everyone. That you just let me leave.

COLLEEN. I *couldn't* go. I *wanted* to. I put on my bathing suit and…the rocks, the broken bottles under the bleachers…Everyone would have seen if I'd gone.

JARED. That's not what happened, Colleen.

COLLEEN. It is.

JARED. Then you should have said something.

COLLEEN. What was there to say?

JARED. I don't know. But something. Not this. Not now. Not after all this time.

COLLEEN. I'm not really the one who picked the timing here, Jared. I'm not the one who went on TV and said, "I was with you."

JARED. Well, if I had known this is what you thought, maybe I wouldn't have said anything.

COLLEEN. You knew.

JARED. I did not.

COLLEEN. You *apologized.*

JARED. How could I *apologize* for something I didn't do. And something I didn't even know you *thought* I did – which I didn't do.

COLLEEN. In your letter. You *said* you were sorry. For what happened.

(a beat)

JARED. That's not what I meant.

COLLEEN. You *said...*

JARED. I *meant* I was sorry for the way things ended between us. That I left without saying goodbye. I'm not sorry for anything we did that night.

COLLEEN. Oh.

(They stare at each other.)

JARED. I made love to you that night.

COLLEEN. I shouldn't be here.

JARED. I made love to you.

COLLEEN. I was *crying.*

JARED. I thought it hurt.

COLLEEN. It *did.*

*(They stare at each other a moment. **COLLEEN** walks past **JARED** towards the door.)*

JARED. What do you want me to do?

COLLEEN. I just wanted you to fuck me.

JARED. I can't.

COLLEEN. And I can't make you.

*(**JARED** shakes his head. He looks at her.)*

JARED. You're not going to tell anyone?

(a beat)

COLLEEN. I have to go.

JARED. Colleen –

COLLEEN. It really helped, you know. That you were sorry.

JARED. Yeah?

COLLEEN. Yeah.

(**COLLEEN** *looks at him for a moment.*)

JARED. What do you want me to say?

(*a beat*)

COLLEEN. It was good to see you, Jared.

JARED. Yeah.

(**COLLEEN** *goes out the door, leaving* **JARED** *alone.*)

End of Play

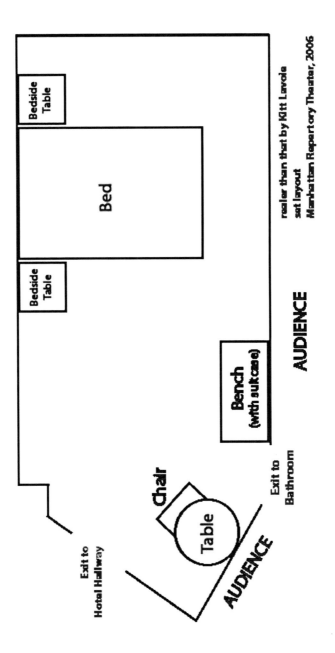

realer than that by Kitt Lavoie
set layout
Manhattan Repertory Theater, 2006

THE STUDENT

by Matt Hoverman

THE STUDENT was first produced by Algonquin Productions at the 34th annual Samuel French Off Off Broadway Short Play Festival at the Mainstage theatre in New York City on July 18, 2009. The director was Suzanne Agins. the cast was as follows:

HUGH SIMMS. . . . . Craig Carlisle

BURT . . . . Steven Hauck

CHARACTERS

HUGH SIMMS – (30s-40s), a writing teacher, a trifle heavy.

BURT – (50ish), a businessman in a suit, perhaps a bit pixiesh.

SETTING

A high school classroom, which is being used to offer evening classes to adults.

TIME

An evening at the end of the class "semester," just before the winter holidays.

ABOUT THE AUTHOR

Matt Hoverman has written three collections of ten-minute comedies: *In Transit* (2006 FringeNYC Outstanding Playwriting Award), *Christmas Shorts* (which includes *The Student* – 2009 Samuel French OOB Short Play Festival Winner) and *Searching for God in Suburbia* (which was a semi-finalist for the 2008 O'Neill Festival and includes *The Collectors* and *Beddy-Bye* – 2006 & 2007 finalists for the Actors Theatre of Louisville's Heideman Award.) He is also the co-book author of *The Audience* (2005 Drama Desk Award nomination for Outstanding New Musical), and the sole author of the full-length comedies *Who You See Here*, *The Marriage Of Moss & Moonlight*, *The Martyr Of Fairfield County* and more. He has been produced or developed by Naked Angels, The Huntington, The Transport Group, The Barrow Group, The Lark, The Axial Theatre Company, The Vital Theatre Company, Algonquin Productions – and was a 2008 Edward Albee Foundation Fellow. As an actor: Yale Rep, The Acting Company, La Jolla Playhouse, etc. UCSD: MFA in Acting; Brown University: BA in Playwriting. MattHoverman.com

(In the darkness, a cheerful Christmas jingle. Then, lights up, music out. We see:)

(A classroom. **HUGH***, a writing teacher in a corduroy jacket, talks on his cellphone. It's a high school classroom, so his desk is adult-sized, but the student's desk/ chair combo is a little small.)*

HUGH. *(on phone)* Hey honey, just one more student conference and then I'm home. What's with the tone? Oh my god. A letter came for me today from *Harper's*, didn't it? I knew it. What does it say, I know you opened it. No, you don't have to read it. I know it by heart. "Thank you very much for giving us the opportunity to read 'Beer Goggles' and for your patience in hearing from us. We receive thousands of submissions a year and do our best to read them all. Unfortunately, we do not have a space for 'Beer Goggles' at this time." And then there's a hand-scrawled note at the bottom that says, "Keep submitting, Hugh!" NO NOTE? Okay, Merry Christmas! Fuck *Harper's*! Fuck them! I'm fine. I'll see you later. Right after I destroy this one last student. Bye.

(In a foul mood, **HUGH** *goes to the door, opens it and speaks off.)*

Enter at your own peril.

*(***HUGH** *sits. Enter* **BURT***, a businessman, in a suit, carrying a business shoulder bag. He's very uptight and has a reverence for his teacher.)*

BURT. Hello, Mr. Simms. Merry Christmas.

HUGH. Yeah, yeah. Fuck Christmas.

BURT. *(sits in the small chair/desk combo, hurriedly pulling out a notebook)* Is this a writing exercise?

HUGH. What?

BURT. I'm referring to your unorthodox teaching style. Do you want me to do a ten-minute free write on the theme of "Fuck Christmas"?

HUGH. No, no. *(considers it)* Actually – *(decides against it)* No. Don't do that. Let's just talk. I'm sorry, Burt. I'm in kind of a foul mood today.

BURT. Use it.

HUGH. What?

BURT. That's what you tell us to do, right, Mr. Simms? Start with how we're feeling in this moment. Don't deny the body. The body tells you what to write.

HUGH. Yeah, just between us, that's bullshit, Burt.

BURT. I don't think so.

HUGH. It is, Burt. It's bullshit.

BURT. You're just testing me or something.

HUGH. No. No, I'm not. I'm leveling with you for the first time all semester. I don't know what the fuck I'm talking about. I'm a hack. And no one wants to read my writing. And you were foolish to sign up for a class taught by someone who doesn't know what the fuck he's talking about.

(beat)

BURT. Do you want me to write for ten minutes about that?

HUGH. No, Burt, no. I want you to see the truth about me. I'm a failure. I know nothing. I have nothing to impart. Nothing to give you. I have no wisdom, no technique, no skill. Any advice I give will probably destroy your story and ruin any chance you have of ever seeing it published anywhere. I'm an anti-teacher, do you see that? I am not a mentor. I am a de-mentor. I will destroy the budding artist within you.

(short beat)

So, let's go over your story, shall we?

BURT. Um, okay.

HUGH. *(paging through a manila folder)* Now let's see, which rough diamond belongs to *Burt?*

BURT. Mine's called "Simon the Gay Elf."

HUGH. *(still looking)* "Simon the Gay Elf"...

BURT. I don't want to be published.

HUGH. What?

BURT. I didn't sign up for this class to write a story to get it published.

HUGH. You didn't? Why not?

BURT. I came to this class because I wanted to learn how to tell a story. My story. Well, I mean, first I came because I got laid off and my employment coach suggested it would be a good way to work on my storytelling skills. She said, when interviewing for a new position it's important to be able to frame your experience as a compelling, empowering narrative. So that's why I signed up. But then I got you as a teacher and my – priorities changed.

HUGH. What do you mean?

BURT. Well, you told us to write what was in our heart.

HUGH. And – ?

BURT. And, so I wrote what was in my heart.

HUGH. *(finding **BURT***'s story)* "Simon the Gay Elf."

BURT. Yes.

HUGH. You wrote about a gay elf.

BURT. Yes.

HUGH. One of Santa's little helpers is queer.

BURT. Yes, that's the premise.

HUGH. Aren't they all gay?

BURT. No, you'd think so, but apparently it's quite a stigma.

HUGH. You've done research?

BURT. In my imagination.

HUGH. Are you gay, Burt?

BURT. Absolutely not. Why do you ask?

HUGH. You said you wrote what's in your heart.

BURT. I'm happily married. But I have a – a *feeling* for men who like other men. Especially very, very small men who like other men.

HUGH. I think they call that pederasty.

BURT. No, not children –

HUGH. You like midgets.

BURT. No.

HUGH. Dwarves.

BURT. No.

HUGH. Little people.

BURT. No, elves. I like elves. I like magical, helpful, pointy-shoed homosexual elves.

HUGH. Okay. Let's deal with this piece structurally.

(*tiny beat*)

Does your wife know you like gay elves?

BURT. I showed her the story.

HUGH. What did she think of it?

BURT. She didn't like it very much.

HUGH. No, I'll bet not.

BURT. She's sort of angry at you, actually.

HUGH. Me, why?

BURT. I told her you told me to write it.

HUGH. I don't remember assigning –

BURT. You told me to open a vein in my arm and stick the pen in it and let the river of my spirit flow out onto the paper.

HUGH. That does sound like me.

BURT. You're my favorite teacher. Ever.

HUGH. Okay. Okay, let's talk about this story. I'm actually kind of glad to hear you say you're not aiming at publication, because I was confused by the intended audience. At first, it seemed like I was reading a fairy tale for kids, but then it got pretty graphic.

BURT. What part was graphic?

HUGH. The part about Simon's gigantic penis.

BURT. That's actually real.

HUGH. More imaginative research?

BURT. No, I looked it up. A human dwarf can have shrunken arms and legs and other organs that are regular sized. And because the rest of their body is so small –

HUGH. It makes the penis seems gigantic by comparison.

BURT. That's what I read.

HUGH. So you're just trying to educate the kids.

BURT. No, this isn't for young audiences.

HUGH. I didn't think so, no.

(HUGH *takes a moment to read a passage of the story to himself.* BURT *looks at him admiringly.*)

BURT. *Your* hands are small.

HUGH. Hm?

BURT. *(changing the subject)* What did you think of my portrayal of Santa?

HUGH. Well, he wasn't very jolly!

BURT. No, he wasn't.

HUGH. He seemed kind of conflicted.

BURT. Yes, he is.

HUGH. *(reading)* I – thought it was interesting that Simon chose Santa Claus, to lust after someone so inaccessible.

BURT. Yes, that is the tragedy of Simon the Gay Elf. He can never express his longing.

HUGH. One of the notes I had was that I wasn't sure why Simon was so obsessed with Santa Claus. I mean, why wasn't he going after Gunther the Burly Elf who worked the bellows in the blacksmith shop, or Hercule the Glass-Blowing Elf? These seem like much better matches for Simon. Why does he fall for a fat old married guy?

BURT. Because his love is impossible, Mr. Simms. It will undo his whole life, the whole fabric of the elf code. He had to bury his desires so long ago. It's only when he gets fired from his job as an accountant at the candy cane processing plant that he has the time to think about his life and the direction it's taken. It's only then that he is open to chance, and to the happy accident of running into Santa in the reindeer stables. Of course he would fall for Santa. Santa is the giver of gifts, the believer of possibility, the maker of magic. Santa is the one who lets him ride on Rudolph and when he asks, "But how will I know where to steer him?", Santa replies, "Just follow your heart." How could he not love him? With everything he has inside of his little elf body – with the big gigantic penis?

HUGH. Burt, do you know I'm married?

BURT. Yes, to Mrs. Claus.

HUGH. Do you know I'm straight?

BURT. Yes, and so am I.

HUGH. But I'm really straight.

BURT. I won't hold that against you.

HUGH. Burt, –

BURT. I wrote this story for you, Mr. Simms. I wrote this story for you. I think you're brilliant.

(*Beat.* **HUGH** *takes in the compliment.*)

HUGH. Thank you.

BURT. Do you see the story?

HUGH. Yes.

BURT. Do you see me?

HUGH. Yes, I do, Burt. Thank you. It's a beautiful story.

BURT. And it's sad too, isn't it?

HUGH. Yes, it is.

BURT. But it's true. It's real.

HUGH. Yes, Burt, it's real.

BURT. You believe in Simon the Gay Elf?

HUGH. Yes, I do. I'll never forget him.

BURT. Thank you, Mr. Simms. Merry Christmas.

(**BURT** *hands him a gift-wrapped box and rises to go.*)

HUGH. Burt, call me Hugh.

BURT. I'd rather not. I need the distance.

(Exit BURT.)

(HUGH dials his cellphone.)

HUGH. *(on phone)* Hi. I'm sorry about before. I was just disappointed. I'll be home in a few. Do you need anything?

(HUGH opens the box, there's a Santa Claus hat inside it. He looks at it for a moment.)

Oh, you know student conferences. They're a little tiring. But they're important.

(He puts on the Santa hat.)

When you're a teacher.

(blackout)

(more jolly Christmas music)

End of Play

(Note: I suggest you make BURT's gift box a narrow, rectangular box, so that the audience suspects the gift inside is phallic. The Santa Claus hat can be rolled up inside it, so when HUGH pulls it out of the box, it unfurls for a nice comic reveal.)

THUCYDIDES

by Scott Elmegreen and Drew Fornarola

THUCYDIDES was first produced at the 34th Annual Samuel French Off Off Broadway Short Play Festival by Geek Ink on Thursday July 16th. The performance was directed by Dev Bondarin. The cast was as follows:

SOLDIER. . . . . Pierce Cravens
STUDENT . . . . Marshall Pailet
PA ANNOUNCEMENT . . . . .Virginia Bryan

CHARACTERS

SOLDIER
STUDENT
PA ANNOUNCEMENT (voiceover, may be prerecorded)

"A nation that draws too broad a disticntion between its scholars and its
warriors has its thinking done by cowards and its fighting done by fools."
- *Thucydides*

ABOUT THE AUTHORS

Scott Elmegreen's shows include *COLLEGE The Musical* (NYMF Award for Excellence in Writing; Richard Rogers Award finalist), and *Vote for Me: A Musical Debate* (commissioned by Aged in Wood Productions). As resident composer of The Assembly, Scott composed for *What I Took in My Hands* (Ontological-Hysteric Incubator; Brick Theater); *Daguerreotype* (Abingdon Theater); *We Can't Reach You, Hartford* (Bedlam Theater; Fringe First nomination); and Joyce Carol Oates' *Tone Clusters* (Fringe Report Award, Best Play). Scott is a graduate of Princeton University.

Drew Fornarola is a composer, lyricist and playwright living in New York City. Writing credits include *COLLEGE The Musical* (NYMF Award for Excellence in Writing, Richard Rodgers Award finalist); *Uncle Pirate* (Vital Theatre Company); *The Adventures of Claudio and Luís* (opening July 2010, commissioned by the New Musical Development Fund); *Vote for Me: A Musical Debate* (commissioned by Aged in Wood Productions); and *Thucydides*. Drew is a recent graduate of Princeton University and member of the BMI Workshop. www.drewfornarola.com

(Lights up on Greater Rochester International Airport, Gate B-2. The set consists of four connected airport waiting chairs. In the first sits **STUDENT,** *a 19 year-old Princeton student dressed in jeans and a sweater, with a button down underneath. He has a Jansport backpack on the floor between his feet. The second chair is empty. In the third chair is* **SOLDIER,** *a 19 year-old E2-Private in the Army, wearing his uniform. In the fourth chair is Soldier's military-issue backpack.)*

PA ANNOUNCEMENT. Attention passengers waiting to board Continental Express Jet flight thirty-two sixty-one with service from Rochester to Newark. This flight will be delayed approximately thirty minutes while we de-ice the plane, and is now scheduled for departure at 10:10am. Thank you for flying with Continental, and we do apologize for this inconvenience.

*(***SOLDIER*** sighs and shifts in his seat. He is holding a* Maxim, *but begins flipping pages slightly too fast to be reading it. To* **STUDENT:***)*

SOLDIER. Fuckin' planes, right?

*(***STUDENT*** has ear phones on, is reading a library book, and does not notice* **SOLDIER.** **SOLDIER** *continues talking to* **STUDENT.***)*

Sucks.

STUDENT. *(looks up)* Sorry?

SOLDIER. Flight's delayed.

STUDENT. Oh. Yeah. Gotta love Rochester weather. *(goes back to his book)*

SOLDIER. Where ya headin'? After Newark, I mean.

STUDENT. Uh, back to school.

SOLDIER. College?

STUDENT. Yeah, second semester.

SOLDIER. You like it?

(**STUDENT** *nods, still reading.*)

I don't think I would like it.

STUDENT. *(stops reading, looks up)* Where're you headed?

SOLDIER. Back to Iraq.

STUDENT. Oh. Wow.

SOLDIER. Got me on a fifteen month deployment over there. They send you home half way through, so…

STUDENT. You're from Rochester?

SOLDIER. Oh yeah. Family's all here.

STUDENT. For the holidays?

SOLDIER. Yeah, well, they're always here.

STUDENT. You going straight back?

SOLDIER. Well, from Newark I go to Baltimore, to Andrews –

STUDENT. The Air Force Base.

SOLDIER. Yeah, fly from there to Germany.

STUDENT. Wow.

SOLDIER. Then Germany to pick-a-stan.

STUDENT. Pakistan?

SOLDIER. No, pick-a-stan – any of them. Then we…

(more quietly)

we go in from there.

(Pause. Wanting to change the subject)

What school do you go to?

STUDENT. Oh. Just a…small liberal arts school in Jersey.

SOLDIER. What, Rutgers? TCNJ? I've heard of schools, you know.

STUDENT. Uh. Princeton, actually.

SOLDIER. Princeton? Fuck.

(excitedly)

You ever see "A Beautiful Mind"?

STUDENT. *(a small laugh)* No.

SOLDIER. That was a great movie.

STUDENT. Yeah I've heard good things.

SOLDIER. Does it really look like that?

STUDENT. What?

SOLDIER. Princeton. You live in, like, a castle and shit?

STUDENT. Oh.

(laughs)

Well, that's it in the movie.

SOLDIER. Wow. Bet you meet a lot of smart people there.

STUDENT. *(shrugs)* Meet a lot of rich people there.

(pause)

Sure, they're smart, too. How about in the Army?

SOLDIER. Best guys in the world.

STUDENT. That's great.

SOLDIER. *(pause)* Must've worked hard in high school, huh?

STUDENT. Sorry?

SOLDIER. To get into Princeton.

STUDENT. Oh. Uh. I don't know. Yeah, pretty hard, I guess.

SOLDIER. You grow up here, too?

STUDENT. Mm-hm, graduated from Brighton.

SOLDIER. Ah, suburbs guy!

STUDENT. Yeah, you?

SOLDIER. John Marshall.

STUDENT. In the city.

SOLDIER. Yeah.

(pause)

What do you study at Princeton?

(STUDENT *slides over into the empty seat next to* **SOL-DIER. SOLDIER** *looks at him.)*

STUDENT. Uh, Classics. Like, you know…

(SOLDIER *starts laughing.)*

What?

SOLDIER. *(joking)* What are you gay or something?

STUDENT. *(pause)* What?

SOLDIER. *(continuing the joke)* Hoping our knees touch?

STUDENT. *(missing the joke)* I couldn't hear, you were talking – !

SOLDIER. *(laughs)* Chill out, man. I'm kidding. And even if you were –

STUDENT. I'm not.

SOLDIER. It's just, like, you know, the movie theater rule.

STUDENT. I don't...know what that is.

SOLDIER. You go to the movies with a guy, you leave a seat between you. Put the popcorn in the middle. So no one thinks you're on a date.

STUDENT. I...think you just made that up.

SOLDIER. *(laughs)* So classics.

STUDENT. Yeah.

SOLDIER. *(pause)* Classic what?

STUDENT. Oh. Classical studies. Like Ancient Greek and Roman history, and literature, culture and languages...

SOLDIER. Hm.

STUDENT. Yeah, it's...fascinating. Actually, we do a lot of military history too, like parallels between Roman society and American...We look at why the empire rose, and fell, and...you know, that kind of thing.

SOLDIER. That's cool. I never liked history, though. I was a math guy. Good at math.

STUDENT. Oh yeah? What kind of math?

SOLDIER. *(not understanding the question)* What *kind* of math?

STUDENT. Like. I don't know. Calculus, algebra...

SOLDIER. The...numbers kind of math. I liked the, you know...

STUDENT. Yeah, yeah. Sorry. Never mind.

(pause)

You scared to go back?

SOLDIER. Nah.

STUDENT. I'd be terrified.

SOLDIER. It's all money in my pocket. Nineteen grand a year!

STUDENT. Nineteen thousand dollars?

SOLDIER. Not bad, right? And the food is free!

STUDENT. So…you like it?

SOLDIER. It's not for everybody. I'm trying to convince my brother to join. He's gotta get out of Rotten-chester, see the world. Mom doesn't want him to, but we'll see.

(pause)

You ever been outta the country?

STUDENT. Yeah, I've traveled a bit.

SOLDIER. Where you been?

STUDENT. Uh, mostly around Europe, I guess. Just, you know, family trips and stuff.

SOLDIER. Family trips to Europe?

STUDENT. I guess, yeah.

SOLDIER. I was in Dubai a few months ago. Friend a' mine got shitfaced, he was pukin' all over the bathroom. And they had one of those, what do you call them?

(**STUDENT** *shrugs.*)

One of those boodays or something, you know, you wash your –

STUDENT. Bidet, yeah, yeah.

SOLDIER. He starts spraying water from it all over the place, trying to clean up, and he's laughing, this whole time –

STUDENT. This is in Dubai?

SOLDIER. Yeah. And I'm like, dude, this is effing Dubai. They're gonna kill us!

STUDENT. Sounds like our parties at Princeton.

SOLDIER. *(laughs)* Yeah, sure.

STUDENT. What?

SOLDIER. Bunch a smart people there.

STUDENT. We still drink and – do stupid stuff.

SOLDIER. Like what, forget to study?

STUDENT. I saw a kid at a party fall out a third story window once.

SOLDIER. On purpose?

STUDENT. No, not on purpose. Lost his balance peeing off a balcony. Dan's just a fuck up.

SOLDIER. How does a fuck up get into Princeton?

STUDENT. I dunno, people are fuck ups.

SOLDIER. Yeah, but not at Princeton.

STUDENT. Turns out Princeton's still filled with people.

(short pause)

SOLDIER. So, did he die, or what?

STUDENT. Broke his back.

SOLDIER. Lucky.

STUDENT. Doctor said the only reason he lived was that he was too drunk to tense his muscles during the fall.

SOLDIER. No shit.

STUDENT. I swear to God. You'd think something like that would change a person. I'm pretty sure he wasn't even off the Vicodin when he came out partying again.

SOLDIER. Jesus.

STUDENT. No one else took it seriously, either. People called him "Defenestrated Dan" when he got back. Now he drinks in the basement.

SOLDIER. *(pause)* Wasn't Rumsfeld a Princeton guy?

STUDENT. Yeah.

SOLDIER. General Petraeus, too.

STUDENT. *(embarrassed, quickly changing the subject)* But that Dubai thing, though. I always figured they wrung all that stuff out of you guys by the time they sent you off.

SOLDIER. They do their best. We're still 19 though.

(pause)

I mean, we get breaks, you know? And they're paying us all that money.

STUDENT. Nineteen grand a year.

SOLDIER. Straight into my pocket. No tax when I'm over there. And a lot of guys got their reenlistment bonus already, so when we get a day off...we're rap stars. Just...throwing money at shit!

STUDENT. I never thought about it.

(pause)

SOLDIER. Forty grand, that bonus. Sixty if you say you'll disable bombs!

STUDENT. But...then you have to disable bombs.

SOLDIER. Yeah, no one seems to wanna do that...Sounds like a pretty good deal to me, though.

(pause)

Haven't told my mom yet.

STUDENT. That's hard.

(pause)

SOLDIER. So how do you find time to fall out a window at Princeton?

STUDENT. What do you mean?

SOLDIER. Even if you are a fuck up, I mean, you must have to study, like, a lot, right?

STUDENT. Oh. Yeah. Well, I dunno. I mean, not *that* much.

SOLDIER. Like how much would you say?

STUDENT. I dunno. It's a lot of reading.

SOLDIER. I bet.

STUDENT. Like...say you've got five classes in a semester.

SOLDIER. That's it?

STUDENT. Yeah, but in the classics department, let's say you've got about three hundred pages of reading per class, so that's like, fifteen hundred pages a week, if you do the math. Plus papers and weekly assignments and quizzes and tests and all that.

SOLDIER. Shit.

STUDENT. Add extracurriculars, and clubs, and community service, and lectures, and seminars…it's actually physically impossible. It can't be done. Probably I pull one or two all-nighters a week, more around exams.

SOLDIER. You'd be a hell of a soldier.

STUDENT. *(laughs)* No. That's…nothing, compared to what you have to do.

SOLDIER. I mean, if you don't need sleep like that. That'd be, like, amazing in the Army. You guys all robots or something?

STUDENT. *(laughs)* Kinda. Robots that run on Red Bull.

(SOLDIER *laughs*)

And Ritalin.

SOLDIER. Ritalin?

STUDENT. Yeah, some people use it to concentrate longer.

SOLDIER. My little brother takes that shit, and he isn't reading any *(looks over at the book in* STUDENT*'s lap)* Socrates. *(He pronounces it SOH-crayts.)*

STUDENT. *(smiles, noticing but choosing not to point out the mispronunciation)* Yeah, it does different things to different people. It's crazy stuff. I don't use it though.

SOLDIER. That's good, man. Not a cheater, huh?

STUDENT. Nah. I'm just afraid to try it.

(pause)

SOLDIER. Don't see so much Ritalin in the Army. It's not so hard to concentrate, there.

(laughs)

Lot a' antidepressants, though. Lot a' antidepressants.

STUDENT. Really?

SOLDIER. And sleeping pills.

STUDENT. Yeah. Must be loud over there.

SOLDIER. You're all trying to stay up, we're all trying to fall asleep.

STUDENT. I got some Catullus I could loan you, that'll knock you out.

SOLDIER. You need a prescription for that?

STUDENT. Catullus is a roman poet.

SOLDIER. Ah.

(pause)

Been a long time since I read a book.

STUDENT. Yeah?

SOLDIER. Maybe middle school. We read some good shit in middle school.

(SOLDIER laughs.)

Then we got to *The Scarlet Letter*. That book sucked.

(STUDENT laughs)

Did me in. Read fifteen pages and said "That's it. I'm done with books."

STUDENT. *(laughs)* I kinda liked *The Scarlet Letter*.

SOLDIER. I hate you.

(They both laugh.)

STUDENT. Well, hey, you're an expert on things I could never learn.

SOLDIER. *(shrugs)* I don't have the brain for that history stuff.

STUDENT. Well, you know a lot of other things.

SOLDIER. Oh, yeah, I mean…

(pause)

I can sharpen a knife so you can shave with it. I can assemble an M-4. Clean it and fire it and shit. And I probably know, like, six hundred and eleven ways to kill an Arab.

STUDENT. To kill a *person*.

SOLDIER. Yeah, I guess.

(longer pause)

I'm gonna grab a hot dog or somethin'. You want anything?

STUDENT. Oh, yeah, umm, I'll have a Balance Bar and a bottled water.

SOLDIER. *(laughs at the order)* Watch my stuff, OK?

(SOLDIER exits. STUDENT goes back to his book for a minute, but isn't interested in it. He looks around. He takes SOLDIER's Maxim out of the top of his backpack and flips through it. Is intrigued. He hastily puts it back as he sees SOLDIER returning.)

(SOLDIER returns with the food. He throws STUDENT the water bottle and sits.)

Here ya go.

STUDENT. Thanks.

SOLDIER. *(reading the Balance Bar label)* All they had was "Pomegranate Blueberry Antioxidant Blast." Hope it's OK.

STUDENT. *(reaches for his wallet)* How much do I owe you?

SOLDIER. Don't worry about it.

STUDENT. No, seriously.

SOLDIER. *(defensive)* Look. I can afford to buy you a Balance Bar!

(SOLDIER holds out the Balance Bar. Pause. STUDENT takes it.)

STUDENT. Thanks.

(They eat for a while.)

STUDENT. Do you ever worry…
I don't mean this to be offensive…but…did you ever wonder…

SOLDIER. *(mouth full)* Nope.

(They laugh.)

STUDENT. Alright, but do you think, when it's all over, it will have been worth it?

SOLDIER. Whadaya mean?

STUDENT. I mean, all things considered, the death toll, the money, everything.

SOLDIER. To stand up for America and freedom?

STUDENT. *(quickly)* Of course. I mean, but do you think we're doing that? Do you think we've really made things better over there?

SOLDIER. *(good-naturedly)* Fuck you asking me for? That's why we got guys like you.

STUDENT. *(pause)* What?

SOLDIER. Guys like you, from Harvard and Princeton and places where Presidents come from. To make sure we're doing it right.

STUDENT. That's a lot of faith to put in a bunch of kids with popped collars.

SOLDIER. Well you ain't passin' it off on me.

(**STUDENT** *eats.*)

(**SOLDIER** *laughs.*)

Anyway, when you guys screw up we've still got God.

STUDENT. *(Pause. Then, good-naturedly)* Of course the other side believes it has God, too, so…

SOLDIER. No.

STUDENT. Well, yes they do. That's at the core of the whole jihadist –

SOLDIER. *(interrupting)* They don't.

STUDENT. *(going on, oblivious)* That's what it's based on. That God is impelling them to –

SOLDIER. *(more angrily)* He's not with them, he's with us.

STUDENT. *(finally sensing **SOLDIER**'s anger)* Oh, I'm not saying…

SOLDIER. He can't be with them *and* with us, and he could never be with them, because if he was, then he wouldn't be God.

STUDENT. OK, I'm just saying…

SOLDIER. And God is God, and God is good, and we are good, and they are fucking evil and so we're killing them.

STUDENT. But maybe –

SOLDIER. All of them, if we have to.

STUDENT. *(giving in)* OK.

SOLDIER. OK. Sorry.

STUDENT. It's fine.

(They eat.)

STUDENT. I just don't think I could do it.

SOLDIER. What?

STUDENT. Kill somebody.

SOLDIER. C'mon, there's a million ways!

(goofing around, acts out all of these things, and mocks "stacking" the bodies)

Knife, throat, dead Arab.

(stacks body)

Hair, spleen, dead Arab.

(stacks body)

STUDENT. *(visibly uncomfortable)* Oh God!

SOLDIER. Chin, twist, dead Arab.

(now laughing)

Grenade, pants, run run run, dead Arab.

STUDENT. OK, stop! Jesus Christ!

SOLDIER. *(still laughing)* What?

STUDENT. First of all, dead person. Dead *person*. Second of all, I...

(They stare at each other. **STUDENT** *sees something in* **SOLDIER** *for the first time.)*

Well, I guess you've gotta laugh about it, right?

SOLDIER. Sure.

(They finish eating.)

STUDENT. I'd just...I think I'd see the guy there in front of me, and I'd know I've gotta shoot him, and I'm all ready to go and pull the trigger or whatever. And all of a sudden I would start thinking, I dunno, maybe this person has a dog, or something.

SOLDIER. *(deadpan, unimpressed)* This Arab you're shooting has a dog.

STUDENT. Jesus. Yes.

(SOLDIER laughs a little.)

Like, maybe he has this dog, and this dog really loves the guy and relies on him every day to feed him and walk him. Maybe this hypothetical dog sits under the hypothetical dinner table and the guy sneaks him little pieces of...kebab.

SOLDIER. Kebab?

STUDENT. Don't they eat kebab there?

SOLDIER. I have no idea.

STUDENT. OK, well, then...and then maybe I shoot the guy, and the next day this dog is looking all over for him but he can't find him anywhere, and I think of this dog's big, sad eyes, and wonder about down the chain who's relying on the dog, and interdependence, these things that transcend culture and humankind...

(SOLDIER looks confused, STUDENT is grasping for an idea he can't quite wrap his head around either.)

I'd just be afraid – I mean, Cicero wrote that...

SOLDIER. Buddy.

STUDENT. What?

SOLDIER. You're afraid of a lot, aren't you?

STUDENT. *(smiles)* I guess so.

SOLDIER. It's not that complicated. Say I have orders to take out a target.

STUDENT. So, to kill a guy.

SOLDIER. *(He looks a little unsettled, but it passes quickly.)* OK. But say I get orders to blow up this target, and I go and I do it. Boom. Easy. Wasn't my decision. It's not on me.

STUDENT. But you were the one who killed him.

SOLDIER. Kinda, not really.

STUDENT. But...

SOLDIER. Maybe someday, if I get to be an Officer…

STUDENT. But by that logic, couldn't you still just…pass responsibility off on the Lieutenant or whoever your superior was by then?

SOLDIER. Oh. Yeah, I guess so. So when I get to be *him,* then.

STUDENT. But then you'd just blame it on the Privates again! No one ever has to take responsibility –

(**STUDENT** *suddenly cuts out in the middle of his sentence, completely distracted by something stage left.*)

SOLDIER. What?

STUDENT. Sorry. *Really* hot girl.

SOLDIER. *(Looks over, catches sight of her.)* Wow.

(*Their eyes follow "her," in perfect synchrony as she slowly "walks" from stage left to stage right, and as she exits, their heads tilt slightly to the left in unison. A pause.*)

You're still gay.

STUDENT. Fuck you.

SOLDIER. You have a girlfriend?

STUDENT. No.

(*pause, then defensively*)

I'm between relationships!

SOLDIER. Look, man, whatever, it's cool.

STUDENT. Well fine, then, what about you?

SOLDIER. Nothing right now.

STUDENT. But, they do have girls and stuff there, right? I mean –

SOLDIER. Yeah, yeah, course they got girls. Not so romantic, though. You know, with the…dying and stuff.

STUDENT. They say fear's an aphrodisiac.

SOLDIER. *(rolls his eyes, smiles)* Christ.

STUDENT. They've done these tests where a woman stands on a sidewalk and gives her number to a bunch of guys, and then she stands on a suspension bridge or something like that, where people would be a little on edge. And the guys she meets on the bridge are always much more likely to call.

SOLDIER. They teach you that at Princeton?

STUDENT. *(pause)* Yeah. But I've noticed it too. Like, I was on this ski lift once with this girl, and I actually did give her my number, and –

SOLDIER. At Princeton, they teach you – out of a book – how to get laid.

STUDENT. Well, no, not – I mean, yes, but…it's just –

SOLDIER. *(a mix of amazement and pity)* Amazing!

(They are laughing.)

STUDENT. I mean, in the classics you see this, too. These great, fantastic love stories, all throughout history, they're always about war. Look at *The Odyssey, War and Peace…*

SOLDIER. I'll put those on my list after *Maxim* and *The Scarlet Letter.*

STUDENT. *(laughs)* Well, you never did like history.

SOLDIER. Yeah. Never liked it.

STUDENT. It's just, with everything you're going through. I mean, I'd think you would, though.

SOLDIER. Nope.

STUDENT. Like, these great empires from the past, you know. They went through a lot of the same stuff we're going through.

SOLDIER. They didn't have terrorism.

STUDENT. I mean, they kinda did.

SOLDIER. Yeah?

STUDENT. So…Rome was like dominating the world in the second century, right?

SOLDIER. OK.

STUDENT. And then at the end of the third century, they fight this fifty year long war with the Sassanids, these guys in Iran, that really stretches them thin, militarily, and financially.

(SOLDIER is laughing.)

What?

SOLDIER. "Sassanids."

STUDENT. Yeah, so this war, the Romans win it, right, but they have to spend huge amounts of money. Then the Germanic tribes, like the Vandals and the Visigoths...I think it was the fifth century. They started attacking the Empire kinda randomly, at the corners.

SOLDIER. *(laughs again.)* The "Vandals," huh?

(pantomimes spray painting)

"Rome Sucks" on the Coliseum and stuff.

STUDENT. *(laughs)* I don't know, maybe, but the point is that Rome, weakened by this long war in Iran, suddenly had to deal with this new, unpredictable, untraditional threat that could strike from anywhere at any time.

SOLDIER. How'd that work out for them?

STUDENT. *(pause)* Not great.

(SOLDIER shrugs.)

You know...that would be really useful stuff to know if you were fighting a war in the Middle East.

SOLDIER. Yeah.

(pause)

And totally useless if you're sitting in a castle in New Jersey.

(long pause)

PA ANNOUNCEMENT. Good Morning, this is the pre-boarding announcement for flight thirty-two sixty-one to Newark. Thank you for your patience. Passengers with small children, and any passengers requiring special assistance, should come to the front desk at this time.

STUDENT. You ever heard of a guy named Thucydides?

SOLDIER. Nah, man.

STUDENT. He was a scholar in ancient Greece, probably the first real historian.

(pause)

I just – made me think of this thing he wrote:

(pause)

"A nation that draws too broad a distinction between its scholars and its warriors has its thinking done by cowards and its fighting done by fools."

(Long pause. Finally, **SOLDIER** *laughs.)*

SOLDIER. That guy calling me a fool?

(They laugh.)

STUDENT. *(contemplatively)* I don't know.

PA ANNOUNCEMENT. We'll now begin general boarding for flight thirty-two sixty-one with service to Newark. Boarding from the back of the plane. Passengers seated in rows twenty and higher, twenty and higher, may board at this time.

SOLDIER. Well, that's me! All the way in the back.

(getting up, zipping up his backpack)

Where're you sitting?

STUDENT. *(***STUDENT** *looks at his boarding pass.)* Up front. Second row.

*(***SOLDIER** *smiles.)*

SOLDIER. Course you are. Cool. Well, good luck, man.

STUDENT. Yeah. You too.

*(***STUDENT** *stands and initiates a handshake, and then* **SOLDIER** *pulls him in to a "frat hug" – hands remain locked in handshake, right shoulders meet, left arms wrap briefly. After a moment, they part.)*

SOLDIER. *(laughs)* You're so gay.

STUDENT. Stay safe, alright?

SOLDIER. Yeah man.

STUDENT. And…thanks. For, what you, uh…

*(***SOLDIER** *cuts him off with a hand gesture.)*

(STUDENT nods, then SOLDIER nods.)

(SOLDIER exits.)

PA ANNOUNCEMENT. Now boarding rows twenty and higher. Rows twenty and higher for flight thirty-two sixty-one with service to Newark.

(STUDENT sits again, puts his book away, zips up his backpack. Blackout.)

JUST KNOTS

by Christina Gorman

JUST KNOTS played at the 34th Annual Samuel French Off Off Broadway Short Play Festival on July 19th, 2009 at the Mainstage Theatre in New York City. The production was directed by Jocelyn Sawyer.

DENNIS . . . . Stuart Luth
PATTY . . . . .Bonna Tek

CHARACTERS

DENNIS: 20s-40s. Proprietor of "Just Knots".
PATTY: 20s-40s. A potential customer.

TIME AND PLACE

Today. A kiosk in a mall.

For Eric

ABOUT THE AUTHOR

Christina Gorman's play *American Myth* was developed at The Public Theater, where she is a member of The Public's inaugural Emerging Writers Group and where it was recently presented as part of The Public Theater's Spotlight Series. The play was also named finalist for the Princess Grace Award and presented as part of the 2010 HotINK Festival. *Split Wide Open* has been produced at the Summer Play Festival in New York City and was developed with a fellowship from Ensemble Studio Theatre through its New Voices Program. The play was also named runner-up for the Princess Grace Award. *DNA* has been produced at Prospect Theatre Company, Hangar Theatre, Samuel French Short Play Festival, and in New York International Fringe Festival, where it received the award for Overall Excellence in Playwriting. *Keep the Change*, co-written with Joy Tomasko, has been produced by the Women's Project for the World Financial Center's Word of Mouth Festival. Her work has also been developed through The Drama League, Lark Play Development Center and the Juilliard School.

(A free-standing kiosk in an indoor mall. DENNIS, unassuming, sincere, stands at his post. He wears a short sleeved dress shirt with a name tag clipped to it. The sign on his kiosk says "Just Knots.")

(PATTY enters. She wears a simple dress and carries a purse. She eyes the kiosk.)

PATTY. Excuse me. Do you sell thread?

DENNIS. *(directing her elsewhere)* Yarn Barn.

PATTY. Rope?

DENNIS. Dick's Hardware.

PATTY. Floss?

DENNIS. Ballard's.

PATTY. Don't you have supplies?

DENNIS. We have no inventory.

PATTY. You don't sell products?

DENNIS. We're a service organization. Our low overhead affords us optimum adaptability in relation to the fluctuating needs of the marketplace.

PATTY. By providing nothing.

DENNIS. We believe active consumer participation via user-generated product results in increased consumer control and therefore greater customer satisfaction.

PATTY. So you don't sell knots.

DENNIS. We don't sell knots, per se. We sell our ability to tie knots. We sell our expertise. Bring us a ligature of any kind, and we'll tie it for you.

PATTY. Ligature?

DENNIS. We're equally adept at manipulating both natural and synthetic fibers.

PATTY. What kind of knots do you tie?

DENNIS. We offer a wide array of knots: granny, half hitch, square, overhand, sheet bend, halyard, clove hitch, cleat hitch, round turn, bowline, tautline, figure eight, sheep shank…we have a brochure.

PATTY. *(looking over the brochure)* Glossy.

DENNIS. Every knot we tie comes with a money-back guarantee.

PATTY. For how long?

(without waiting for an answer)

Do you have a sample of your work?

(He takes out a thin rope.)

DENNIS. *(holding up the rope)* For demonstration purposes only. Not for resale.

(as he ties)

Known as a fisherman's knot for its usefulness in tying fishing line, this knot is best used for joining two ligatures of slippery surface and/or of similar diameter.

(He holds up the tight fisherman's knot, then grabs the two ends and pulls, which easily loosens the ends, almost like a magic trick.)

PATTY. How'd you learn to do that?

DENNIS. Self-taught. I – like knots. Always have. It's just a… well…

PATTY. Ladybugs. I collect ladybugs. Anything with ladybugs. So, like that.

DENNIS. Yes. Only I don't *collect* knots. I don't have them, you know, hanging around.

PATTY. Right. Of course.

DENNIS. *(conversation stalls)* So, um, miss…

PATTY. Patty.

DENNIS. Patty. Is there something…

PATTY. Oh! Oh, yes.

(She takes from her purse a chiffon scarf. Dennis watches it billow as she pulls it through the air and onto the counter.)

PATTY. *(cont.)* I'd like a square knot, please. My mother used to tie them for me, but she…

*(**PATTY**'s voice trails off, as talk of her mother is painful for her. **DENNIS** notices.)*

DENNIS. Of course.

(He picks up the scarf to begin to tie it.)

PATTY. Wait.

*(She takes the scarf and puts it around her neck, holding the ends of the scarf out to him. **DENNIS** ties the knot for her, keeping a respectful distance.)*

How does it look?

(He pulls out a small mirror and holds it up.)

Oh, oh. It's lovely. How much do I owe you?

DENNIS. A dollar fifty.

PATTY. That's all?

DENNIS. Square knot. Category: simple. Also called a reef knot.

(She takes a small gift box and ribbon from her purse and slides it on the counter.)

PATTY. It's for my neighbor. She takes care of my cat.

(meaning the ribbon)

My mother was really good at bows too.

DENNIS. Oh. We don't do bows.

PATTY. Why not? Because it's a bow, not a knot?

DENNIS. No, no, it's a knot. It's a bow knot, or a bow tie knot, actually. We're not supposed to…
Are you familiar with the "ladies" at gift wrap? Over by the food court? Last Christmas, they accused us of unfairly stealing their market share.

PATTY. What? But that's –

DENNIS. I know! Capitalism, free market economy, fair competition, right? We were forced to sign a non-competition agreement regarding bows of luminous or semi-luminous ligatures. So you take this on over to them; I'm sure they'll be thrilled to take care of you.

(under his breath)

Charge you twice as much...

PATTY. But...I want you to do it.

DENNIS. I'm sorry. I wish I could.

PATTY. But you do...you do such good work.

(He considers. He takes the gift on the sly. She stands guard in front of him, blocking the view of the "ladies at gift wrap." He ties the bow and slides the gift to her. She beams; he blushes.)

DENNIS. On the house.

PATTY. Oh no, I couldn't –

DENNIS. I insist. Can't charge you for it anyway. There's no code in the system for semi-luminous bows.

PATTY. All right then. But I do owe you for my lovely square knot.

(sliding the money across the counter towards him)

Five dollars. There you go. *Five* dollars.

(He bashfully nods in thanks. They look around to be sure the Gift Wrap Brigade isn't watching.)

Thank you,

(looking at his nametag)

Dennis.

DENNIS. Thank you for your business.

(noticing the pattern on her scarf)

Hey. Ladybugs.

PATTY. *(smiling)* See you soon.

DENNIS. Always welcome. We pride ourselves on our high percentage of repeat customers.

(She exits. **DENNIS** *stands behind his counter, waiting for customers. He takes a fast food cup from under the counter and sips from the straw. He puts the cup back. He takes out the piece of rope and practices a particularly intricate knot.)*

*(***PATTY*** *re-enters. She's carrying a large shopping bag labeled "Dick's Hardware.")*

DENNIS. Welcome back!

(From the shopping bag, **PATTY** *pulls a thick, coiled rope and lands it with a THUD on the counter.)*

PATTY. I'd like a slipknot, please.

DENNIS. For?

PATTY. Um…

DENNIS. What for? What, what do you need a slipknot for?

PATTY. Sorry, but is that for you to know?

DENNIS. Oh, well –

PATTY. Does the reason for purchase need to be determined in order to complete the transaction? Because you see it doesn't say anything about that in your brochure so I was under the impression –

DENNIS. No, no, you're correct. It's not company policy to ascertain the product's – use. I just…I don't know if I can.

PATTY. Can?

(reading from the brochure)

"…knots of *any* kind…"

DENNIS. *(clarifying)* Should.

PATTY. Well if you won't make it –

DENNIS. Tie it.

PATTY. Tie it. I thought since someone's going to do it, it may as well be you.

DENNIS. Why me?

PATTY. Is there a law against making a noose, owning a noose? Using a noose?

DENNIS. Well there's a law against *that.*

PATTY. Since you won't be using it, you don't have anything to worry about.

DENNIS. I...I wouldn't want to be held responsible –

PATTY. This is a business transaction. There's no blame here. It's as if you're selling me a...a gun.

DENNIS. A gun?

PATTY. For my protection.

DENNIS. A slipknot is not normally an instrument of defense. I'd be an accessory. To whatever you...

PATTY. If you do your job right, I won't tell. I'm here for your expertise. I trust you.

(**DENNIS** *takes in her meaning. Considering, then...*)

DENNIS. *(with difficulty; business tone)* Type? Strangle-snare knot, scaffold knot or hangman's knot?

PATTY. Oh, I didn't know there were...whichever one has the best – craftsmanship.

DENNIS. Hangman's then.

(**PATTY** *watches intently as* **DENNIS** *ties a hangman's knot. It's like watching an artist at work. When he's finished, he lays the noose gently on the counter. They look at it, neither moving for a moment. As soon as* **PATTY** *goes to reach for the noose:)*

That'll be four hundred dollars.

PATTY. Four hundred dollars?!

DENNIS. Special order. Not in our brochure. And you're in a rush. You *are* in a rush? Rush job. Emergency mark-up.

PATTY. But you tied it in no time.

DENNIS. Thank you.

PATTY. Would you have tied it slower if it wasn't a "rush job"?

DENNIS. I would've tied it later.

PATTY. You have other orders to fill?

DENNIS. No.

PATTY. But I don't have four hundred dollars.

> (**DENNIS** *picks up the noose and moves it away.*)

> You do accept credit!

> (**PATTY** *lays a credit card on the counter.* **DENNIS** *picks up the card.*)

DENNIS. For nine ninety-five, would you like to purchase our extended warranty?

PATTY. It doesn't have to hold for very long.

DENNIS. You'd be surprised.

PATTY. *(holding his gaze, then:)* No thank you.

> (*He hesitates, about to run her credit card.*)

DENNIS. I'm sorry, I'm unable to perform this service for you at this time.

PATTY. Why? Is there something wrong with my card?

> (*understanding he's refusing*)

> All right. I would like my rope back. Untie it, please.
> I'll have to figure it out for myself.

DENNIS. No no! Don't do that!

PATTY. Why not?

DENNIS. It's dangerous! There's no quality control! You could get hurt. I mean hurt. Just hurt. Do you wanna just hurt? Protractedly? I mean, you don't want to suffer, right? You've suffered enough, presumably, or you wouldn't need me to...to...

PATTY. ...help.

> (*He runs her credit card. She signs.*)

DENNIS. We should conduct a test. Quality control.

> (*He has her put her arm in the noose. He yanks, pulling the noose tight around her arm. It's violent. She yelps. He waits. Her face tight, she slowly removes her arm from the noose. She holds out her shopping bag. He places the noose into it.*)

(She hesitates. She might stay. He might say something. She turns to leave.)

DENNIS. *(cont.)* May I interest you in our in-home service? Contact us and one of our representatives will bring "Just Knots" directly to you. In the event you find you need a knot tied in your own home.

PATTY. For what?

DENNIS. Clove hitch? Two half hitch? Tautline? Selecting a knot with the proper friction and load bearing weight is – crucial.

*(**PATTY** starts to exit. She stops, looks at the pamphlet.)*

PATTY. It says here I can call for an appointment. If I call, who will come?

*(**DENNIS** takes the pamphlet and writes on it.)*

DENNIS. Call that number. You'll get me.

(She takes the pamphlet, then turns to leave.)

You'll call?

PATTY. I will.

DENNIS. You will?

PATTY. I will.

(sincere, touched, meaning it)

I will.

*(**PATTY** exits. **DENNIS** returns to behind his counter. He discovers **PATTY**'s credit card. He looks in **PATTY**'s direction, considering calling her back. Instead, he slowly slips the card into his pocket.)*

(Lights fade.)

End Play

OFF-OFF-BROADWAY FESTIVAL PLAYS

THIRTEENTH SERIES
Beached   A Grave Encounter   No Problem   Reservations for Two
Strawberry Preserves   What's a Girl to Do

FOURTEENTH SERIES
A Blind Date with Mary   Bums   Civilization and Its Malcontents   Do Over
Tradition 1A

FIFTEENTH SERIES
The Adventures of Captain Neato-Man   A Chance Meeting Chateau Rene
Does This Woman Have a Name?   For Anne   The Heartbreak Tour
The Pledge

SIXTEENTH SERIES
As Angels Watch   Autumn Leaves   Goods   King of the Pekinese Yellowtail
Uranium   Way Deep   The Whole Truth   The Winning Number

SEVENTEENTH SERIES
Correct Address   Cowboys, Indians and Waitresses   Homebound   The Road
to Nineveh   Your Life Is a Feature Film

EIGHTEENTH SERIES
How Many to Tango?   Just Thinking   Last Exit Before Toll   Pasquini the
Magnificent   Peace in Our Time   The Power and the Glory
Something Rotten in Denmark   Visiting Oliver

NINETEENTH SERIES
Awkward Silence   Cherry Blend with Vanilla   Family Names   Highwire
Nothing in Common   Pizza: A Love Story   The Spelling Bee

TWENTIETH SERIES
Pavane   The Art of Dating   Snow Stars   Life Comes to the Old Maid   The
Appointment   A Winter Reunion

TWENTY-FIRST SERIES
Whoppers   Dolorosa Sanchez   At Land's End   In with Alma
With or Without You   Murmurs   Ballycastle

TWENTY-SECOND SERIES
Brothers   This Is How It Is   Because I Wanted to Say Tremulous   The Last
Dance   For Tiger Lilies Out of Season   The Most Perfect Day

SAMUELFRENCH.COM

OFF-OFF-BROADWAY
FESTIVAL PLAYS

TWENTY-THIRD SERIES
The Way to Miami   Harriet Tubman Visits a Therapist   Meridan, Mississippi
Studio Portrait   It's Okay, Honey   Francis Brick Needs No Introduction

TWENTY-FOURTH SERIES
The Last Cigarette   Flight of Fancy   Physical Therapy   Nothing in the World Like It
The Price You Pay   Pearls Ophelia   A Significant Betrayal

TWENTY-FIFTH SERIES
Strawberry Fields   Sin Inch Adjustable   Evening Education   Hot Rot
A Pink Cadillac Nightmare   East of the Sun and West of the Moon

TWENTY-SIXTH SERIES
Tickets, Please!   Someplace Warm   The Test   A Closer Look
A Peace Replaced   Three Tables

TWENTY-SEVENTH SERIES
Born to Be Blue   The Parrot   Flights   A Doctor's Visit
Three Questions   The Devil's Parole

TWENTY-EIGHTH SERIES
Along for the Ride   A Low-Lying Fog   Blueberry Waltz   The Ferry
Leaving Tangier   Quick & Dirty (A Subway Fantasy)

TWENTY-NINTH SERIES
All in Little Pieces   The Casseroles of Far Rockaway   Feet of Clay
The King and the Condemned   My Wife's Coat   The Theodore Roosevelt Rotunda

THIRTIETH SERIES
Defacing Michael Jackson   The Ex   Kerry and Angie   Outside the Box
Picture Perfect   The Sweet Room

THIRTY-FIRST SERIES
Le Supermarché   Libretto   Play #3   Sick   Pischer   Relationtrip

THIRTY-SECOND SERIES
Opening   Circuit Breakers   Bright. Apple. Crush.
The Roosevelt Cousins, Thoroughly Sauced   Every Man   The Good Book

THIRTY-THIRD SERIES
F*cking Art   Ayravana Flies *or* A Pretty Dish   The Thread Men
The Dying Breed   The Grave   Juniper; Jubilee

SAMUELFRENCH.COM

OTHER TITLES AVAILABLE FROM SAMUEL FRENCH

THAT PRETTY PRETTY; OR, THE RAPE PLAY
Sheila Callaghan

Comedy / 2m, 3f

A pair of radical feminist ex-strippers scour the country on a murderous rampage against right-wing pro-lifers, blogging about their exploits in gruesome detail. Meanwhile, a scruffy screenwriter named Owen tries to bang out his magnum opus in a hotel room as his best friend Rodney ("The Rod") holds forth on rape and other manly enterprises. When Owen decides to incorporate the strippers into his screenplay, the boundaries of reality begin to blur, and only a visit from Jane Fonda can help keep worlds from blowing apart.

Sheila Callaghan's *That Pretty Pretty; or, The Rape Play* is a violently funny and disturbing excavation of the dirty corners of our imaginations.

"A submersion in the anarchy of ambivalence: variously a rant, a riff, a rumble - about our notions of naturalism, objectification, perversity, and beauty...There's sass and sarcasm in Callaghan's high-energy punk writing."
- John Lahr, *The New Yorker*

OOHRAH!
Bekah Brunstetter

Dramatic Comedy / 4m, 3f / Interior Set

Bekah Brunstetter makes her Off Broadway debut in September 2009 at the Atlantic Theatre Company! Ron is back from his third and final tour in Iraq, and his wife Sara is excited to restart their life together in their new home. When a young marine visits the family, life is turned upside down. Sara's sister is swept off her feet; her daughter Lacey trades her dresses for combat boots, and Ron gets hungry for real military action. In this disarmingly funny and candid drama, Bekah Brunstetter raises challenging questions about what it means when the military is woven into the fabric of a family, and service is far more than just a job.

"The young scribe's talent and potential are obvious in this Southern-basted dramatic comedy about the war mystique as it plays out on the American home front..."
— *Variety*

"...Poignancy and terrific humor in both the writing and performances..."
— *Theatremania.com*

SAMUELFRENCH.COM